4GB Hundred Rupees

...... a flight through time

Shambu Jayachandran

VISHWAKARMA PUBLICATIONS VP

4GB Hundred Rupees
...... a flight through time

First Edition : May 2016
© Author

ISBN 978-93-83572-93-9

Published by:
Vishwakarma Publications
283, Budhwar Peth, Near City Post,
Pune - 411 002.
Phone No: 020 20261157
Email: info@vpindia.co.in
Website: www.vpindia.co.in

Cover Design, Typeset & Layout
Meghnad Deodhar
Vishwakarma Publications.

To the Empty Words and Wounded souls

Thanks To

The Almighty who looks after me!

D S Santhosh Kumar, who remains the first reader and editor, and inspiration for my book. DS Suresh Kumar, for his support in my career and Academics.

Rev. Fr George Mathew Karoor, for his love and care. My loving teachers : Shiny Pappachan, Rajeena Joseph, Dr. PJ Jacob, Ann Kristenne Moreira, Prof. JA Thomas, Dr. George Mathew and Shirley Stewart. Gayathri Mohan, for her suggestions and support at all stages in the writing of this book. Cinu Mary, Bavitha MK, Kabani R, Soumya Chandran, Anand V Cyjo, Shani John, Reshma Kuriakose, Rose, Veena MG and Meenu for their love and care which motivated me a lot.

My loving mother S D Sindhu Devi, grandmother Savithri, Sister Lekshmi, brother in law Vijayashekar and my Nephew Viswanath for being in my life.

My aunties, Cousins, colleagues and friends who supported me all the way.

The loving people of Kerala and Kolkata

My extended family on Twitter and Facebook.

Connect the Author:

Facebook Profile	: www.facebook.com/shambumariner
Facebook Fan Page	: www.facebook.com/shambuahead
Twitter	: www.twitter.com/shambuahead
Website	: www.shambuahead.com
Blogspot	: www.shambuahead.blogspot.com
Gmail	: shambuahead@gmail.com

CHAPTER
O N E

The plane was descending on Kolkata. Looking down her window Amy caught a glimpse of the river, the mighty Hooghly, meandering its way like a muddy silver serpent alongside the city spread out in millions of fluorescent dots. Her hands moved up to touch her chest, an old habit she picked up as a little girl, emulating her aunt perhaps, a spontaneous homage paid to the river Goddess. A silent prayer came out of her heart. Her eyes felt wet; she shut and opened them a few times to prevent the drops from rolling down. The plane touched down on the runway.

****

The officer on the counter stamped her passport without asking any questions. Amy moved towards the luggage conveyor. She didn't have to wait long. Picking up her brown polo bag and bluish grey suitcase she proceeded towards the pre-paid taxi booth.

Her cell was ringing... Avinash.

'Oh you have landed at last!' The relief was evident in her cousin's voice, 'we came to the airport, but they could not tell the exact arrival time. We waited till ten, me and Shruti. Couldn't wait any longer, Tania was alone at home. Can you wait in the lobby for half an hour? I am coming.'

'No, no! You don't have to come.' Amy tried to dissuade her brother, 'I'll take a taxi.'

'It's late. It won't be safe for you to take a cab all alone.'

Amy laughed. 'I am not a young girl anymore Avi! And has our city become so unsafe that a woman can't travel alone at night?'

'O.k. take a cab then.' Avinash relented at last. 'It shouldn't take you more than half an hour, the roads are empty now. We'll be waiting for you.'

Amy was relieved. It had always bothered her that someone should wait for her for hours standing in front of the arrival lounge in absolute boredom counting every minute. But more importantly she wanted to savor the last phase of her journey through her hometown in solitude, in the dark rear of the cab without being disturbed by questions that she knew would be asked again and again once she reached home... and if possible could she visit... there's a long queue in front of the taxi counter too. Amy decided to take the cab from outside. Contrary to her expectations she was not immediately surrounded by competing cab drivers. Maybe things have improved or maybe it's too late... She stopped a cab, a black and yellow Ambassador, trademark Calcutta taxi - a living symbol of timelessness. The driver, a young boy hardly nineteen popped his head out.

'Gariahat jabe?' Amy asks. The driver nods.

'Koto?'

'Five hundred, Madam!

"Five hundred!" Amy stared blank at the driver. Five hundred? How? Inflation was it? Or devaluation of the Indian Rupee? Time had passed she knew, but five hundred! It was twenty... well, it couldn't remain twenty of course. She is not that naïve to think it would still remain twenty after twenty-six years. She had estimated two hundred, three hundred maybe. But five... Was she being cheated?

The driver must have read the agony on her face. 'Can't take the bypass Madam, it is closed for repairs,' he said almost apologetically in an effort to explain the fare just demanded, 'we have to go by Shyambazar, Dharmotolla.'

What bypass was he talking about? She didn't know any bypass. It was always V.I.P, Ultadanga, Sealdah or DumDum, Shyambazar, Dharmotolla. Where was this bypass? She wanted to know but didn't ask. She didn't want the driver to know that she had come to the city after so many years.

'Alright. Take my luggage.' She moves in.

The old Ambassador. Dear old Ambassador; the bulky car with retro looks, shining steel bumpers and round headlights. It had remained the same, hadn't changed a bit. Amy felt the seat with her hands. The same sofa-like seat, never failing to relax. She pulled down the glass to the full to let the breeze in. It was hot and humid but the breeze generated by the speeding cab caressed her face lessening the discomfort. She looked out. It seemed like a ghost town. The roads were empty. Not a single shop was open. Even the restaurants were closed. Nothing was moving on the streets except a lone vehicle or two.

'This city is a good girl, she sleeps early' Soham had joked on an earlier homebound journey like this many years back. They were coming from Mumbai, her in-law's place. The plane from Mumbai arrived late.

Amy looked on enchanted. Her city... Her very own beloved city, sleeping under the orange-yellow light of sodium vapor lamps... she seems so tired, worn out. The emptiness of the night had bared her scars, potholes like gaping wounds filled with rain water, overfilled garbage vats in front of closed markets, stench of fish and flowers rotten and mixed up, in the solitude of night she lies licking her wounds in silence like an old suffering bitch. The bright neon lit billboards with smiling faces had failed to provide any comfort. The buildings on which they hang are dark, dilapidated, with plasters falling off, unhappily holding up promises of an impossible, all smiles future. The disconnect was palpable. Facelifts had failed to hide the lines of the ageing, unwilling bride; the past had firmly held its ground, shoving the future higher up, nearer to the sky, where it floated unsure of itself knowing very well it was impossible to come down and touch the present... Amy's eyes fell on the shadowy figures lying on half lit pavements in front of closed shutters. Men women children sleeping still, like corpses abandoned in the battlefield of life watched over by howling dogs engaged in battles of their own.

Suddenly Amy felt sad and depressed. The sight seemed unbearable, she wanted to close her eyes but didn't, kept on looking. Why did she feel like this? The sight was not new to her. As someone born and brought up in this city she had seen this so often almost every day and hadn't cared bit, passed by naked children and half naked women and fully naked lunatics without even noticing as if they didn't even exist, and occasionally had thrown down a coin or two without any feeling of pity, but never before she felt it revolting as she feels now... When she first saw a homeless man in the streets of New York the feeling was exactly the opposite though. She was pleasantly surprised. 'People live in streets here too!' She had said unable to hide her excitement. Soham had laughed. 'There are losers everywhere dear' he had said. Her initial excitement over, she had felt genuinely sad though, not the fleeting sadness she feels now, wondering how one can become a destitute in a land of plenty. It must be much more painful to be a loser in a land full of winners than in a land where very few are. She had told Soham.

'Where are you coming from, Madam?' The driver asked putting a brake on Amy's thoughts.

'America.'

'You live there?'

'Yes.'

'Permanently?'

'Yes..

'For how long Madam?'

Amy hesitated a bit. 'More than twenty five years.' She said.

'Really?' The driver couldn't conceal his surprise, 'But you speak Bengali just like us!'

Amy blushed in the darkness. This was a compliment she is often showered with by her Bengali friends in America almost all of whom are no longer able to speak in pure Kolkatan Bengali. You can forget your mother tongue in three months if you wish and if you don't you won't forget in thirty years.' was her typical response, always said with an air of nonchalance concealing the pride beneath. But now in dark rear of the cab she preferred to keep quiet hoping the cab driver wouldn't be more inquisitive.

'How is life there Madam?'

Amy found herself at a loss of words... How is life... How couldn't one respond to such a question? Whose life? Her life? Or others? People she knew? Or she didn't know? How could she say about others life? How was her own? Could she rate it?... Excellent? No... Good?...

'I mean people earn a lot more there, don't they?'

Ah that's what he meant! Everything becomes so easier to comprehend if measured in terms of money... 'I suppose so.' Amy replied.

'I have friends in Dubai, you know Madam. They drive taxis too but earn ten times more than I do.'

Why don't you go there then? Amy wanted to ask, but remained silent. The driver answered on his own.

'They take only Muslims and Christians in Dubai. I can go there only if I become a Muslim or a Christian.'

Amy remained quiet. The driver got silent too. There was a certain irony in what he said that touched her ... No doubt the lad would earn a lot more if he changed his religion and go to Dubai, his life would change... better clothes, better food... send money home... the repairs long pending, mother's medical expenses, sister's marriage...maybe his own marriage, the girl's father relenting at last. It was his religion that was standing in between. Why couldn't he change it? Why couldn't people change their religion? So many things got changed... countries... habits... surnames... even one's own name... why not religion then? Why was it so difficult to change? Was it because of the Gods?

The car took a turn. It was South end of the city now... Bhawanipore... Hazra... she was getting closer to home ... Suddenly sounds of drumbeat could be heard at a distance...faint at first ... getting louder and louder...A shiver went down Amy's spine. It was a familiar sound! Was it?... The drumbeats got even louder and in a matter of seconds a truck appeared from a side street and whizzed past the cab. 'Bolo Durga Maiki... ' A male voice shrilled out through the beat of the drum...'JOI'...A chorus followed... Amy felt goose bumps all over her... she leaned out of the window for a better look. A group of young men on the rear of the truck surrounding an idol of the goddess with ten hands, her face wrapped up in a piece of cloth. Another beat of the drum ...another truck passed by... four idols in it, smaller in sizes, all had their faces covered... 'Bolo Durga

Maiki..' Another shout rose above the drumbeats followed by even louder 'JOI'... The trucks sped through the empty road, took a turn and disappeared. The beat of drums lingered on...so were the howlings of an agitated pack of dogs...and of their tribes near and far...

'Is it panchami today?' Amy asked.

'Yes Madam,' the driver replied enthusiastically. 'Tomorrow is shashti, and its puja from Monday. Don't you know?'

Amy didn't respond. She didn't know. She had forgotten this time... for the first time in her life she has failed to remember its puja season; the biggest festival of the Bengalis. It had never happened before, not a single year had passed in her long stay in America that she had not remembered the dates, had always marked them beforehand on the calendar, sometimes on the September page, sometimes on the October page and counted the days... but she didn't mark them this year, it didn't cross her mind for once that puja is coming. OniOindrilla had occupied every thought of hers, every moment she thought only of her, nothing else...

Something caught her eye. A street sign...

'Stop the car!' Amy yelled.

The driver brought the car into a screeching halt.

'What is it maam?'

'Move back a little,' Said Amy, 'I want to see something.'

The driver put the car on reverse gear and drove back.

'Stop!' Amy instructed. She looked out of the window. There... the green arrow shaped sign sticking out of a lamppost, pointing left... Kolkata Police Hospital – the letters read.

An overwhelming sense of fear surrounded Amy. She felt her hands turn cold... The thought that she had been trying to block away from her mind had surfaced up once again and this time she made no effort to put it away.

'How far is Kolkata Police Hospital from here?' She felt her voice trembling as she asked the driver.

'Not very far MMadam. About five minutes from here.' The driver replied.

'Can you take me there?'

'Now MMadam? Didn't you say you want to go to Gariahat?' The driver didn't try to hide the surprise in his voice.

Amy hesitated for a moment. What should she do? Go home first then come tomorrow with Avinash? Or should she... No, she would go to the morgue right now. The hospital was so near... she should settle the matter right now.

'I have some work there. Won't take more than ten minutes.' She told the driver.

'Ok MMadam, as you wish.' The driver moved his car towards the left side of the road.

Amy's heart began to beat very fast. For the last thirty-six hours, whenever the thought of that news had appeared at the corners of her mind she had blocked it by thinking of something else, some fond memories of OniOindrilla or something totally different. Soham's instructions on thought control had come handy, not for once she allowed herself to dwell upon it, but now it had numbed her totally, the hollowness inside her stomach was becoming unbearable...

The news had come on Thursday at one o' clock in the afternoon, when she was sitting on OniOindrilla's bed listening to Norah Jones' song that she listened night and day. Avinash had called. A body of a young girl had been lying unclaimed in the morgue of

Kolkata Police Hospital for the last three days. The body was found in a back alley of a Central Calcutta neighborhood that was the den of foreign tourists, mainly backpackers. The face was completely distorted and unrecognizable, burnt with acid. No documents were found. Avinash who knew about OniOindrilla's sudden disappearance, and the fact that she had come to India and may have come to Calcutta too, thought that there might be a possibility that the body was of his niece. But since the face was unrecognizable he couldn't make out anything. So he called and gave her the information. Her initial reaction was hysteric but then Soham convinced her with his irrefutable logic that the probability of the body being OniOindrilla's was one in ten million and there was absolutely no justification in making herself a nervous wreck before she went to Calcutta and took a look at the unclaimed corpse. All through her journey from New York to Calcutta she had been practicing the mind control techniques that Soham had taught her, effectively blocking the thought that the unclaimed corpse might be her daughter's. She had intended to visit the morgue tomorrow after reaching home with Avinash at her side, but now all her plans had gone topsy-turvy, knowing that the hospital was so near she no longer was able to block the dark lurking thought off her mind. She needed to find out who the girl was and she needed to find out right now.

' Kolkata Police hospital has come MMadam.'

Amy felt a jolt inside her chest.

The driver had halted the cab in front of a red brick building; Kolkata Police Hospital the signboard at the gate read.

Amy felt her legs totally numb. She tried to move but her legs wouldn't budge.

'Madam?' The driver said sensing the silence at the rear.

Amy made a huge effort to bring herself out of the stupor, opening the cab door, and came outside.

'I will be back soon.' She told the driver.

'Shall I come with you MMadam?' The driver said noticing the white face and trembling voice of his passenger.

'No need.' Amy said and walked towards the gate alone. The lobby was near empty, a couple of ward boys in green uniform and a nurse in white were chatting. The receptionist at the counter was busy, his eyes fixed on the Onitor screen. He looked up noticing the lady approaching.

'I want to go to the morgue.' Amy came straight to the point.

A frown appeared on the receptionist's forehead.

'A body was brought here by the police last Thursday. Post Mortem's done but it has not been sent for cremation yet. It's still lying in the morgue of this hospital. I want to know if it's my daughter's body.'

The young man looked at the lady standing before him without trying to hide the surprise on his face.

'Are you alone MMadam?' He asked.

'Yes.'

'Your name?'

'Amy – Amrita Ray.'

Amy brought out her passport from her handbag.

'Here's my passport.'

The receptionist took a look at the document. The surprise on his face became more vivid.

'You are from America MMadam?'

Amy nodded.

'Your daughter had come to India too?'

Amy nodded again.

'Was there any accident?'

'I don't know...'

'What makes you think the corpse might be your daughter's?'

Suddenly Amy felt a rush of blood ascending to her head.

'I just want to see the corpse! Will you please let me see it?' She shouted.

The receptionist startled at her sudden outburst returned the passport and pressed a bell.

A ward boy appeared.

'Take Madam to the morgue,' the receptionist instructed the boy, 'Dr. Mazumdar would be there. Let Madam speak to the doctor.'

Amy followed the ward boy. They went through a door that opened in a long passageway. It seemed like a long tunnel. Amy felt her legs become heavy as she dragged herself behind the ward boy. The passage seemed to be never ending; it looked so old and worn out. The plasters were falling off the wall colored a garish green, the wooden beamed roof had withered with time.

Was it all her fault that the situation had come to this? Had she made a fatal mistake in refusing to accept Randolf? Her dear daughter had fallen in love and she wanted to marry the guy, and it was she who stood in between. She didn't want her daughter to marry an American. She had her own dreams about her daughter... and now all her dreams stood in the verge of being shattered... She didn't expect that OniOindrilla would leave her house... leave her mother... her father. It happened so suddenly, and she gave no time at all, not even an ultimatum. She just left without saying anything... The photo agency she worked with said she had come to

India taking up an assignment... That was three months back. In between she did not get a single phone call from her, not even a mail. She thought of coming to India to find her daughter but she did not know where to go. Even the agency did not know where she was. The last time they heard of her was when she was in Varanasi, that was a about month back. But still she was relieved to know that her daughter was alive... but then on Thursday afternoon this news came... Could it be her? The corpse lying in the morgue? Avinash said it was probably of a girl twenty-twenty two years old - the same age of OniOindrilla... No! No! No! It can't be OniOindrilla! Soham had said repeatedly that there was zero percent possibility that a corpse lying in morgue of a hospital in a city where hundreds die in accidents each day might be of their daughter. And there was no reason to believe that Oni was in Calcutta... No! It can't be her! It can't be her!...

Sound of people crying came to Amy's ears. But she could not see anyone. Then suddenly from the far end where the corridor took a leftward turn some figures appeared a few men and a woman. The woman was wailing being held by two other men who were crying too. A couple of ward boys pushing a cart on top of which lay a body covered in a white cloth. Within seconds they came close and brushed passed. Amy looked at the woman. The woman too looked at her, their eyes met. For a moment she stopped crying, her agony replaced by surprise. The ward boys said something to each other, Amy could not understand what. The group passed by, the wailing faded as they moved out of sight.

Suddenly Amy felt her limbs going weak. She caught hold of the ward boy's shoulder who immediately clutched her putting his arm around her back.

'Are you o.k. Madam?' He said in Bengali.

Amy took a few deep breaths.

'Yes I am O.k.' She said finally.

But the ward boy did not release her from her grip. Neither did Amy try to free herself.

'How far is the morgue?' She asked.

'Just round the corner Madam,' said the ward boy, 'we are nearly there.'

A red door with the words MORGUE written on top of it appeared before Amy's eyes. A cold shiver ran down her spine. It would be her! It would be her! She was sure...

The Boy pushed the door and they were inside. It was a small room with another door on the other end. The boy made her sit on a bench.

'I am calling Dr. Mazumdar Madam. You sit here for a while. Will you be O.K.?'

'I will be o.k.,' said Amy, 'You go ahead.'

The boy went inside through the other door. As he opened the door and got inside, an obnoxious smell hit Amy's nostrils. But that did not bother her much. She had hospital experience and was used to all kind of odors though not necessarily that of the morgue.

Amy waited sitting on the bench. It seemed like an eternity. Twenty-one years of bondage... joys and pains shared together under one roof... would it all come to an end? Would she no longer be able to talk to her daughter... would she no longer be able to hold her in her arms? Would it all end in a few moments from now... Soham where are you Soham? Amy wanted to cry. Why didn't you come with me? Why did you made me face all this alone?

It was all her fault. She should have been more flexible. She should have tried to understand her daughter better. But didn't she try? She tried, she surely tried but failed. How was it possible for her to accept an American as her son-in-law? It was such an impossibility! But she should have accepted the impossible. However painful it might have been.

The smell came again. The door had opened. A doctor in white had appeared with the ward boy.

'I am doctor Mazumdar.' The doctor said, 'How can I help you Madam?'

Amy repeated what she said to the receptionist. The doctor nodded and bringing out a piece of paper and a pen from his apron pocket handed it to her.

'You have to fill this form first Madam.'

Amy took a look at the form and filled it up with her shaky hand, name, address, nationality etc...

She handed the form back to the doctor.

'Come with me,' said the doctor.

Amy rose from the bench. The ward boy moved quickly to hold her by the arm. Amy did not refuse the help. They went through the door into a hall, lined with drawers fitted into the wall. The smell was now revolting. Amy thought she would vomit, taking a deep breath she controlled herself...

On top of every drawer a number were engraved... 3012.. 3013...3014... Amy looked around. Which one was hers?

The doctor stopped before a vertical row with drawers with numbers from 3155 to 3160. Amy felt her heart pounding against her chest. She clutched her fist to in an effort to remain in control.

The doctor stooped low and pulled the drawer marked 3156. Amy closed her eyes. This time the stench hit so hard that Amy thought she'd fall. The ward boy put his arm around her back.

'Have a look Madam.' She heard the doctor saying.

Amy opened her eyes.

No, it is not her!!

Amy immediately knew the body that was lying in the drawer was not of OniOindrilla's. The face was impossible to recognize, it was partly burnt and partly decomposed, but by a look at the rest of the body she knew it was not her daughter. She didn't have to look twice, she knew her daughter too well to have not recognized her at the first look.

She shook her head.

A smile appeared in the doctor's face. The ward boy too could not help a smile.

'Thank God!' The doctor said.

Amy felt tears sliding down her cheek. The turmoil that was going on inside her had ended but still she felt her limbs weak. The boy helped her out of the chamber and made her sit on the same bench in the front room.

'Are you feeling better now Madam?' He asked.

Amy nodded. Yes, she was feeling much better now. The strength on her feet had returned and her heart had stopped pounding. She opened her handbag and bringing out five hundred rupees gave it to the boy. She knew this was not America; this was her motherland where a little expression of gratitude was warmly appreciated. The boy beamed.

'Your daughter will come back to you safely Madam.' He said smiling.

Amy smiled back. She knew the boy said it just to make her feel better but she wanted to believe that he was right. Now that the worst was over things would turn for the better. Her daughter would indeed come back to her.

Coming out of the hospital Amy called Soham.

'It's not her!'

A gasping sound was heard on the other end. She felt the tension wearing off her husband's chest.

'I told you!' Soham exclaimed, 'Don't you worry anymore. She would come back!'

'But I don't want to come back right now Soham,' Amy said, "I want to stay back for a few more days and do some more enquiry.'

'Fine,' Soham agreed.

The driver was waiting. He didn't fail to notice the color back in the passenger's face.

'Is everything o.k. Madam?' He asked.

'Take me to Gariahat now.' Amy said.

She lay back on the seat getting into the cab. The cool breeze caressed her face. Her daughter was still away from her but she felt a sense of joy. Her mind was still crowded with worries and her heart still felt heavy but the darkest worry was over. She could give herself a breather at least for the time being.

****

'Gariahat has come Madam.'

Amy looked up. 'Take the Circular road, the second lane after Purna cinema.' She gave the driver the required instruction.

This was her home turf... Gariahat market... Deshbandhu Medical Stores... Purna cinema... the playground of her childhood and youth... Amy looked on as if in a dream... memories... memories... so many memories... in every inch of the road... There comes Purna cinema, pink colored as ever... she leaned over to the other side without even thinking to take a peek at the posters as she had always done whenever passing the theatre house, to inquire what was the latest picture showing. "Finding Fanny" was the name of the film now showing. Five people – two young and beautiful women, and three men of which two were old men with white hair and one tall and handsome, were standing in front of the car in different postures and varied expressions leaning on it. The two old gentlemen seem to be listening resignedly to something said by one of the young women, while the hero was looking objectively at the other young woman, probably the heroine ... Many a times in her youth she had come to watch movies in this theatre, along with her friends. How long back was that - Nineteen seventy three – seventy four? They watched mainly Bengali and Hindi movies in this hall, that of Uttam Kumar and Suchitra Sen and of Amitabh Bacchan and Rekha. English movies were never put up here, they had to go all the way to Esplanade to watch movies of Marlon Brando and Marilyn Monroe. New Empire and Lighthouse were the two theatres that put up Hollywood blockbusters. They would take a taxi from college, an Ambassador like this. Seven of them would sit in the same car, three in the front pushing the driver to the right hand side door from where he had great difficulty maneuvering, his hands ramming into the girls thighs whenever he pushed the shaft gear. Four of them would squeeze into the rear occupying the space allotted for three. But if Tinni were with them, there would be no space for more than three; the fat chubby girl would alone occupy the space for two. Where were they now? All of her friends? Tinni... Ritu... Shreoshi... Shimul... All of them must be mothers of big children like her now; some might have become grannies too. How time flew by! Once in front of the ladies counter of this theatre she and her friends would stand in queue clutching notes in their hand, being pushed by other women from behind. On reaching the counter, the money had to be transferred to another hand coming out of the mouse hole, and tickets would be given along with the change in exchange. No one could ever see the faces of the men who gave the tickets; only the hands coming out of the mouse hole were visible. The rush in the queue of women was nothing compared to that in the men's queue, in front of the male counter, the two queues being divided by an iron railing to prevent the men from encroaching into women. But that did not prevent the men from passing all sorts of comments that they always had time to utter in spite of the great pushing and fighting going on between them. The same counter, the same mouse hole windows, the same iron railing... only it was empty now. The show had ended, the characters had retired never to come again. Their hair had grayed; lines had appeared under their once youthful eyes... they had given way for the new players to come on stage... for a new show to begin.

'Second lane!' Amy reminded the driver. 'Yes... Go straight and take the third cut to the right!' She couldn't hide the excitement in her voice. Her heart was beating fast.

Her lane! She was born here, brought up here. She played in its dusty asphalt.... Sarat Bose Road ... The buildings on both sides were all two or three stories with little space in between. Amy got a peculiar 'squeezed' kind of feeling. The narrowness is palpable... the buildings from both sides seem to be closing in.

It was strangely quiet now. Not even the dogs were barking; must have gone venturing to some other lane. Only a couple of streetlights were on leaving much of the lane in the dark. Many years ago, on one such quiet night a daughter had stood beneath one of these lamp posts anxiously waiting for her father to return home. Those were the nights when fear was on the air, bursts of pipe-gun fires could be heard at intervals, knifed bodies were found lying in street corners at the break of dawn. But that was many years ago; much water has flowed down the Hooghly river since then, the world has changed... her own world too. But why then... why then entering this narrow stretch she was having the feeling that nothing had ever changed? the same buildings standing in eternal postures, the same narrowness... the same lamp posts... generating more darkness than light as ever? Was the girl still standing beneath the post, still waiting for someone to come back home, her hairs plaited in two long braids tied in red ribbons, anxiety etched in her big dark eyes?

Three decades had passed, and thousands of clouded miles. Amrita had become Amy, few lines have appeared under those big dark eyes ... but did anything change really? The girl inside still preferred to eat with her hands, still hesitated to use fork and spoon, still wore saris with sleeved blouse, still shy of baring her arms, still in company of her own loves to weave her hair in long braids, and she was still waiting for someone to come back home.

'Stop here!' Amy told the driver.

****

Both his brother and sister-in-law - Avinash and Shruti - were waiting at the gate to receive her. Both were ecstatic, the smiles on their faces were undoubtedly genuine; so were the tears on their eyes, coming straight from the heart. The surprise on their faces was genuine too and so was her own surprise discovering the grays of his hairs and the bald on the forehead and the paunch on the bellies. First they were stunned then they were jubilant to hear that she had herself visited to the hospital morgue and made sure that the corpse was not of OniOindrilla's.

Shruti hugged her in delight.

'I knew! I knew it couldn't be OniOindrilla! I went to Kalighat yesterday and prayed to the mother!'

'You have developed guts!' Avinash couldn't help expressing his astonishment and admiration. 'Can you believe, the girl who was so afraid of ghosts is now visiting a morgue all alone in the dead of the night?'

Hours passed sitting in the big drawing room on the second floor as they walked down the memory lane together. So much to say, so much to hear, so many memories to shed tears upon, and so many more to laugh over. When they finally got up it was three in the morning. OniOindrilla was mentioned over and over again, but with interest and warmth. Amy opened her suitcase to bring out the album and showed them her photos and also of her own and Soham's and others.

'How beautiful she looks!' Shruti heaped praises on her niece's features, 'Look at the eyes! Doesn't she have Amidi's eyes?'

'And the nose is of Sohamda's.' Observed Avinash.

'I am dying to meet your Tania.' Said Amy, 'How old is she ?'

'Seventeen.'

'Seventeen! She is no longer a little girl then!'

'Not at all!' Laughed Shruti. 'Just wait till you see her in the morning. She is now taller than me! About to cross her father.'

It was Tania's room they had prepared for her. The room had once belonged to her before she got married and even after marriage she had spent many afternoons here basking in the warmth of Soham's company, never forgetting to carefully lock the door and the mammoth sized windows. A feeling of overwhelming nostalgia swept over Amy... the same old mahogany bed lying on which she had spent hours studying... and reading and daydreaming... and writing..., the same old cupboard directly across the bed where lay hidden her secrets... even the mahogany dressing table remained exactly where it had always remained for God knows how many years. Standing in front of its huge Belgian glass so many afternoons were spent checking the acnes on the cheek, applying Tuhina on the face and arms, trying bras and blouses and saris proud of being the owner of a beautiful and wonderfully curved body ... kotkis, jamdanis, paper silks... and the red colored benarasi she wore on the day of her marriage. Only the computer table and computer under the window were new additions. And that huge jumbo sized poster of Shah rukh Khan pasted on one of the doors of the cupboard. Amy looked at the poster and felt bad for the young teenager who must have left the room grudgingly being forced out by her mother and was sleeping somewhere else, dreaming of her favourite Bollywood star who sadly would not be smiling at her the moment she wakes up in the morning, at least for the next few weeks.

As a young girl she too hated to be evicted from her room but had to consent unwillingly and quietly often as relatives would regularly flow in.

Amy sat on the bed and picked up the photo frame from the side table. She had got her mother's eyes like OniOindrilla; lively, and full of spirit. How time flew by! Amy wondered. Once in this room a young girl kept awake late lying on this bed, pillow under her chest reading Shesher Kobita and fantasizing about her Mita', her that special friend in life who would completely change her world; and now another young girl having finished playing with her Barbies that gather dust above the cupboard, and finishing reading Harry Potters that adorns the shelf, spends her nights looking at the poster of her favorite star who smiled at her from the cupboard door, as if he would step in any moment. Amy puts off the light and lies down. Darkness... more darkness plunged in with eyes closed. The image of the smiling movie star hung above her eyes... Shah Rukh Khan, the present heart throb of millions of young girls in India.

In her time it was Amitabh Bacchan. Her friends were crazy about this 'angry young man' who had taken the movie crazy Indian public by storm surpassing the other heart throb Rajesh Khanna. Her friends were divided over the two; she liked Amitabh better, though she was never crazy over him. Her cousin sister was, and she had pictures of Amitabh cut out from the pages of Anandlok and pasted them on her scrapbook. She would laugh and tease Riya for this juvenile hobby of her's. But when it came to Bengali movies all the girls were unanimous about their adoration of Uttam Kumar, the ultimate Bengali hero with a million dollar smile. Uttam Kumar was dead now and no one knew how old Rajesh Khanna had become but Amitabh Bacchan was still very much in the fray, though over sixty and all his hairs turned gray he was still giving Shahrukh Khan a run for his money. Along with Soham he had seen many Indian movies in America, she had watched several with her daughter too - Shahrukh Khan starrer and Madhuri Dixit starrer - all those movies with lavish traditional Indian settings, about joint families and marriages... Dilwale Dulhaniya... Ham apke hai kaoun... she wanted Oni to get a feel of Indian traditions and values. Oni her darling was definitely impressed by the dazzling costumes that the characters wore and the lavish settings, but with her American sensibilities she never missed to laugh over when without any precursor the hero and the heroine would begin to sing and dance, and the background music begin to play from nowhere. But the most ridiculous to her were the bunch of dancers with funny dresses who would appear behind the couple from nowhere, wearing the most outlandish costumes and would dance in the same funny steps as of the hero and the heroine.

'They are all metaphors, symbolic,' Ami had tried to give an explanation to her daughter, 'You must not take them on face value.'

'What metaphor Ma!' Oni would laugh aloud, 'they are all nonsense! How can sensible people with a sane mind watch such nonsense!'

That made her feel bad. Though funny at times, she never thought such songs and dances as nonsenses and even appreciated many a songs, but she could not totally refute Oni's observation that many such scenes were irrelevant to the story of the movie. Her daughter also found it difficult to understand many situations that were impossible for anyone who was not born and brought up in India to understand.

'Why would the heroine always play second fiddle to the hero Ma?'

She found it difficult to explain to her but also pointed out the good things that were imbedded in the Indian way of life.

Once when Oni observed why someone touched the feet of someone else's, she had explained to her daughter that it was a manner in which younger people showed respect to the elders. And she did not fail to mention that while in India she and Soham too bent down to touch the feet of elders.

'I hope you won't tell me to touch your and dad's feet.' Oindrilla had chuckled.

Oindrilla liked to watch Hollywood and British movies. And also French movies with English subtitles.

'They are realistic Ma!' She would cry out whenever she'd hear her mother criticizing any Hollywood movie, 'Would you ever find any Hollywood star singing around a tree!'

She liked Richard Gere and George Clooney and Hugh Grant and when she was younger Tom Cruise was her favorite... she had a poster of Tom Cruise pasted on her room. It was now replaced by

Norah Jones and others. Oindrilla listened to Norah Jones all the time and told her mother to listen also many a time but Amy never did. She never tried to appreciate western song, as her taste got stuck between Rabindra sangeet and other old Bengali and Hindi songs of her youth. Amy never tried to open her ears to something different. Only when Oindrilla was gone, Amy picked up the CDs lying abandoned in her bedside drawer and played the songs one by one on the Sony Walkman that she had left behind along with everything else.

Spinning, laughing, dancing

to her favorite song

A little girl with nothing wrong

And she's all alone....

Suddenly Amy felt like crying... Why did you leave me my daughter? She wailed within... why did you leave without telling me anything? She had not heard from her for over a month. She neither mailed, nor called...I feel so lonely without you Oni... I feel so afraid!!!

!"!Amy opened the door and came out to the balcony. Dawn was breaking. The sky was all red but the sun was not yet visible; it was still hiding somewhere behind the tall buildings on the opposite side. The air was cool and a soft, refreshing breeze was blowing from the west. Amy looked around. From this balcony in the second floor, the entire lane could be seen. It was still empty and quiet. The dogs were sleeping on the road tired after their night long turf wars. The cats were sleeping too, curled up on top of the walls and over sunsets above the windows. The only sounds were the chirping of birds and the ringing of a distant bell coming from a house at the far end. It was the Bhattacharjees Amy knew, waking up their Gods. They were always the first to wake their gods up. Others would follow soon and many bells would ring out across the lane accompanied with bugle like sounds from conch shells. There – it was blowing from the Bhattachajee house! Amy listened… once…twice…thrice…No more. That was the rule, three consecutive blows. No more, no less… She could never really manage the conch shell. The prolonged sound like a ship's honk is not easy to bring out; all her efforts had gone wasted.

The best she could manage was a little honk, no more than two seconds much to her aunt's dismay – all her efforts to teach the niece to bring out a nice long honk had gone down the drain too. It was a real disgrace because women much older and much younger than her can blow the shell for fifteen seconds at a stretch or even more…. A conch shell blowing competition used to be held every year here in the last day of the puja festival, for the housewives of the neighborhood to showcase their blowing skills. Preeti Boudi was the undisputed champion ….

Memories flooded her mind and the adrenaline rushed at the thoughts of two young girls in pony tails waiting in their school uniform of white shirt and navy blue skirts waiting for their school pool car to arrive and pick them up. Proudly displaying their young budding breasts, they discussed amongst themselves the plump boy and laughed, who nervously looked at them from time to time, obviously showing lack of confidence and readiness to stare at girls of that age and quench their thirst and quest of adolescent queries…. The lightly built handsome young man with gold frame specs and a briefcase in one hand lightly brushing the lips of the beautiful and adorably hot woman at the next house on the doorsteps with a mischievous smile on his lips silently reminding her of the wild night spent together, and then waving good bye to his little girl peeking from the window…Rijumonda…Ami remembered the thrill that she and her cousin had of watching for the first time a man opening up his wife in conjugality…Boys playing cricket on the street and the ball rolling over into the drain...the plump boy now grown up into a strong and sturdy youth running towards the drain to pick up the ball from the drain and bending down to pick it up when he suddenly notices two girls with long hair plaited in two braids walking down the lane wearing sari, and books tightly held to their now fully grown breasts in an effort to cover them up while the boy much bolder now looking at them with admiration... a young boy watching this from his second floor window... a police van stationed at the entrance of the lane, khaki clad officers dragging out young men from their houses and shoving them into the vans in front of their wailing mothers and sisters.... so many images... so many memories down this narrow lane still empty... still quiet...

'Ami na?'

Startled Amy looked up. An old man looking at her from the second floor terrace of the house opposite.... Ganguli uncle! Oh dear, it was Ganguli uncle! Bald and bare bodied as ever. How old he had become!

'Ami na?' The man said again adjusting his high power glasses.

'Ganguli jethu!' Amy said.

'When - When did you come !' The old man nearly shouted.

'Yesterday night.' Amy replied smiling.

'Oh my god! I can't believe! I just can't believe! How many? After how many years?'

CHAPTER
T W O

'Eight years.' Amy replied almost apologetically.

'Eight years! Remembered us after eight years – haan?' The old man kept smiling. 'Your husband... Soham? Has he come too?'

'No.'

'Why? Why didn't you bring him with you?'

'He is too busy with his practice. No time to spare.'

'Ah! Too busy making money! Too busy making money! No time for anything else. I understand.' Suddenly the old man got silent. The smile died down from his face. Amy wondered why.

'What about your children?' Ganguli Jethu was smiling again, 'You have a daughter don't you?'

Amy nodded.

'How old is she?'

'Twenty one.'

'She has grown up then! Has she come?'

Amy heart sank for a moment. She nodded her head to say no.

'Why didn't you bring her with you? It's puja now. She'd have liked it now.'

Amy remained silent.

The old man laughed. 'I understand,' He said wiping his specs with the lungi tied to his waist. 'They have no interest about their motherland. America has become their home.'

Amy felt a bit irritated now. She tried to defend her daughter.

'It's not entirely true,' she said, 'they do have interest but their perspective is different.'

It was true. It would be wrong to say that her daughter had no interest on India at all. It was her mother's land, father's land and she had heard many things about India from her parents. She had learnt to respect some of the values that her parents shared though she might herself not put those in practice and yes she had many questions about the traditions of this land, questions her parents had never asked but should have. Of all places she had come to India for the photo shoot? Why? She asked her boss in the agency whether she was forced to go to India or she went on her own and he said that she was given a choice. Either to go to Brazil to do a feature on the relations between different ethnic communities there, or to go to India and do a feature on the changing socio-economic scenario of the country. She opted for India. Why? Why she did not choose Brazil? It was not that she knew nothing of Brazil. She had Latino friends in her school, and college too. And some of them had Brazilian connections and she knew Latin too, a language she had in her high school. She knew no Hindi at all that was a must to travel around India and rudimentary Bengali, but still she came to India. Was it not because of some kind of the tug she had felt for the land of her parents? She had felt the urge to visit her roots, to see firsthand the things she had heard from her mother since when she was a little girl, was it not for the attachment she had for her mother and the land of her birth?

'I hope you had taught her some of our values,' Ganguli Jethu said,

'Has she become one hundred percent American or retained some of our qualities? Does she dress like all those white girls we see in T.V. – wearing half pants, smoking cigarettes?'

Amy felt quite irritated now but at the same time she wanted to laugh. The old man had got stuck in time where everything he saw was through the prism of typical Bengali middle class sensibilities, where everything that was western or American was bad. What's wrong in wearing half pants? She herself wore jeans while in New York. She never smoked though and she had not let her daughter smoke too, not because she considered it bad to smoke in front of parents as was the notion in India but because it was a health risk. She had made her daughter understood and made her quit when she started smoking after leaving high school. Oindrilla did not disobey her mother as many of her friends often did, it was because of the Indian values she had been able to imbibe upon her daughter.

Amy remembered something.

'Does Jethima eat paan-jarda even today Jethu?' She asked. She had remembered Ganguly Jethu's wife was an addict of jarda or chewing tobacco that she consumed with beetle nuts cut in small pieces and the bottle green colored heart shaped paan leaf.

'Sure she does. At least five paans a day, with extra strong jarda. But why do you ask?'

'Why doesn't she quit. Consuming paan-jarda is as bad as smoking tobacco.'

Ganguli Jethu went silent for a moment then laughed out.

'I got your point! I got your point!' He laughed. 'We are great hypocrites aren't we? Women smoking are bad but chewing tobacco is not!'

'And sexist too!' Amy did not fail to mention.

'Right! Right!' Ganguly jethu chukled, 'Why should smoking be bad for women only, it's bad for men too. Why should men continue to smoke and women smoking considered a taboo? America has changed your outlook I see!'

Amy smiled. She did not even think about it before, what she said just now, about smoking and chewing tobacco. It just came to her spontaneously. He was right. America has indeed changed the ways in which she looked at things while she was in this country.

'How's the political temperature there?' The old man asked, 'Do you think Bush will attack Iraq?'

Amy smiled. 'There's a big possibility.' She said.

'That will be preposterous! They don't have any WMDs. Bush is hatching up a lie. They just want Iraq's oil, it's all about oil!'

'But Saddam Hussein is a tyrant, isn't he. No harm in removing him.' Amy reminded. She felt at ease at last, talking politics at such an early hour was no doubt a bit odd but it was better than talking about children and their progress in life.

'But there are so many tyrants in the world,' Ganguly uncle countered, 'Why doesn't America remove those too? On the contrary they support autocratic regimes all over the world. They even supported Saddam all along till he invaded Kuwait. It's all for oil, and nothing else.'

It seemed so funny to Amy. The sun had not risen yet, in a city thousands of miles away from where it was actually happening, an old bare bodied man wearing only a lungi and a sari clad middle aged woman discussing about the American justification of invading Iraq, or rather the lack of it.

'They won't find it easy, you see. May be they would remove Saddam Hussein but it would be very difficult to keep Iraq under their control. They were saying it on CNN the other night.'

Ah CNN! That was what building the bridge...

'It will be another Vietnam for them. They will have to return red faced. All the experts are saying that.'

Amy looked at the old man in amazement. How things had changed since the days she was here. Satellite T.V. had united the world, and everything that was happening in any part of the world, gets immediately broadcasted all over the world to every house in the planet where there was this idiot box. And now there was the Internet. Not only one could see, one could connect to someone sitting in front of his computer thousands of miles away in some other continent too. All this was unthinkable only two decades back in days of her youth when there was only black and white TV and that too very few. The entire neighborhood would flock to a particular house where there was one, to watch an old movie or a football match. Now it all seemed so remote, those days, like black and white photographs in an old album. What more was to come in the future, that would turn the present day into its monochromatic self, to be stored only in the alleyways of one's memory?

'Will come later sometime and discuss politics with you Ami,' Ganguli Jethu said, 'It's always more interesting to get first hand news! Ekhon choli re will have to go to the bazaar now.'

'So early?'

'If you want the best fish you must go early.' The old man winked. 'Choli re ekhon.'

Ganguli Uncle left. Amy looked down. People had gathered around the tap below with buckets and bottles and metal pots to fill them with the first water supply of the day. They were looking up at her. The news would spread fast. The Bose girl had come from America. And they would come visiting in hoards, the boudies & mashimas; the women of the neighbourhood and none would come to discuss politics. All would be asking the same questions.

The general ones: Where is your daughter? Why hasn't she come? What is she doing? And the more feminine ones: When are you planning to marry her off? Is she having any affair? What do you have in mind, NRI or some Bengali guy from this city? And suggestions: I have a good boy in hand you know, a computer engineer. Earns in six figures, tall and handsome; good family; Just the right match for your Oindrilla.

If only her Oindrilla had to face these women! She would have just got up from her chair and slammed the door without saying a word, a thing she can never do, never could. She had always sat and heard patiently nodding and smiling, smiling and nodding, always agreeing, always careful not to hurt others feelings. Oindrilla despised this patronizing attitude of hers. Why can't you speak out what's in your mind, mom?' She often said.

Why couldn't she? Was it because of her upbringing? Or was it in her genes? Her mother was submissive too, never argued with her husband or her sister – in – law, always letting her opinions being trampled by that of others and her feelings too, torturing her already tortured soul. To friends and relatives she was a paragon of virtue, an embodiment of the ultimate Hindu women, tolerant, virtuous, sacrificing, accepting and never questioning and always smiling. But behind that smile was a tortured soul, did she even realize how tortured she was? Maybe she did. But self-pity had made her accept her shortcomings. Maybe she had become institutionalized like millions of other Indian women who had never learned to question themselves or the world. She too had retained the qualities of her mother. To remain quiet even when forced to listen to something that was not pleasing to the ears just for the sake of not hurting the speaker's feelings. So many times it had happened that she wanted to shut her American friends off knowing they were talking rubbish but she could not, her genes, her culture got in between sealing her lips, numbing her vocal chords.

Coming back into her room Amy rearranged the bed, spreading and tucking the sheet under the mattress, putting the pillows in the right position. She came out of her room and walked up towards the kitchen. A cup of tea was a must now, she was going to make it herself.

Someone was already inside carefully pouring water into the kettle-the cook. Amy watched the cook making tea. This had always been the tradition of their family, all the cooking including the making of tea was done by the cooks, and the serving were done by the women. This had become a problem to her when she got married. Till then she had only cooked once in a while as a trainee to the cook, to learn the essential Bengali dishes that every Bengali girl should know how to prepare and that too under the watchful eyes of her aunt. But she was never in practice, so coming to a new family after marriage, she had to face great difficulties in cooking for the entire family. Her in laws though very much westernized in their outer behavior had retained the tradition that all the cooking should be done by the daughter-in-laws though all the servings were to be done by the servants. And while in America she had to do everything single handedly all the cooking, serving and the washing too. Soham used to help in serving and washing in the early days but then he stopped altogether. For a long part of her stay in America she had to do everything alone till Oindrilla completed her junior school when she began to help her mother, first in serving and washing, and as she grew up in cooking too. Though she was never able to teach her daughter much of cooking Oindrila never hesitated to assist her and also learned how to make tea and rice and lentils.

'Good morning.'

Shruti's voice was heard at the door.

Amy turned back and smiled.

'You up so early!' Said Shruti, 'No jet lag?'

'Where is your daughter? I can't wait to meet her!' Amy asked.

'She is still sleeping.' Shruti replied, 'She doesn't normally wake up before seven.'

The cook left bowing before Amy. Shruti picked up the teapot and poured tea in two of the three china cups on the tray. Handing one to Amy she took the other.

'How is your daughter in her studies?' Amy asked.

'Oh, good. Her grades are fine. But what worries me is her addiction to computers. She is always playing games on it! I don't understand what fun they get playing those silly games! She has become an addict of sorts.'

'Is it so!' Amy was surprised, 'I thought only in America kids are addicted to games!'

'No! No! It's the same here too! Kids no longer read books apart from their text books. They are always surfing the net and playing games and watching T.V. And yes talking to friends over their cell phones! It's so irritating! I don't understand what they talk so much on phone. Can you believe Amidi, we have a library full of books but our daughter doesn't even care to read.'

That was a pity! Amy thought. How could one resist the temptation of such a library! It was her father's, she had spent so many afternoons in its solitude reading fictions and poetries and memoirs of famous personalities. 'Reading builds character' her Baba used to say. She wondered if Shruti read too, normally a child picked up from her parents – the mother especially. She had never abandoned her reading habits and her habit had been passed on to her daughter. Though Oindrilla was always internet savvy but she was an avid reader too, she never missed an opportunity to read a good book.

'May I ask you a question Amidi?'

Amy looked up. She knew what was coming.

'Why did Oindrilla leave?'

No need to beat about the bush, Amy thought. She looked straight into Shruti's eyes.

'She had an affair with an American boy.'

'Oh dear!' Shruti gasped.

'She wanted to marry him. I objected. We had an argument and she left.'

Avinash appeared at the dinette.

'You know why Oni left without any intimation?' Shruti wasted no time to give her husband the piece of news she just received. 'She is having an affair with an American boy, she wanted to marry him. Mother and daughter had an argument and she left.'

'Oh dear!' Avinash dropped himself on a chair.

'A real surprise isn't it?' Shruti quipped.

'Is it true?' Avinash looked at Amy. Amy nodded.

'Dear me! I was thinking day and night why the girl left without telling anybody. So this is the reason!'

None said a word for a few seconds. Then Shruti continued. 'She will come back. I am sure she will come back soon. Don't you worry.'

'I am not so sure' sais Amy, her voice quivering, 'I am so worried.'

Shruti came near and put an arm around her shoulder.

'Maybe I should have agreed.' Amy found difficult to control her voice.

'No! You did the right thing.' Shruti said pressing her shoulder,

'How can you let her marry an American boy? It's impossible. She will come back. She can't stay away for long.'

'Why do you say it's impossible?' Avinash asked, 'Has no Bengali girl ever got married to an American?'

Shruti looked at Avinash as if he had asked a purely juvenile question.

'Are you out of your mind?' She said in an animated tone, 'How can Oindrilla marry an American? Cultural difference issues are bound to creep up and result in a disaster. Is there any dearth of good Bengali boys in America? And if none can be found there, is there any dearth here? Boys will wait in queue for our Oindrilla. No, you did the right thing Amidi,' Shruti turned to Amy, 'just because she is having an affair doesn't mean she has to marry. And if you ask me I would say you shouldn't have let things come to such a pass. You should have intervened much earlier.'

'I didn't have an inkling.'

'That's what I am saying. You should have. You should have known when it all started and nipped it at the bud.'

Amy remained quiet. Shruti's words made her feel worthless an; incapable mother who had no influence upon her child. But she tried. She tried against all odds to dissuade Oindrilla from her intent of marrying Randolf and she got no support from anyone, not even her husband. She was the culprit in the eyes of her friends who found nothing wrong in an Indian girl having affair or marrying an American. There were so many Bengali girls and boys married to native white Americans in America and some of them were her friends, how could she make the arguments for it? She was fighting a lone battle and it went horribly wrong. She had lost her child.

Looking at Amy's worried face Avinash intervened 'But the

question now is how can we find her? 'We just can't sit and wait for her to return. Are you sure she has come to India?'

'Yes.' Amy confirmed.

'How can you be so sure?'

'I contacted the magazine she is working for. She has taken up an assignment with them on something. In fact I checked with the immigration authorities. She had left for Delhi on nineteenth August.'

'Don't they know where she will be staying in India?

'Not really. They have given her a free hand, she can shoot wherever she likes.'

'But she must be in touch with them?'

'No! That's why I am so worried.' Amy cried out, 'She didn't contact them yet! She had last called them on the ninth of the last month!'

'Oh dear!' Shruti's hand went up to her mouth.

'I am so afraid,' Amy broke down. 'What if something...'

'No. No. If something bad had happened, you'd have got the news. In our country if something happens to a foreigner it immediately gets reported.' Avinash said in an assured voice. 'Her visa must have expired hasn't it, unless of course she has extended it.'

'Can't we know that? Amy asked.

'Sure we can. I will go to the visa office tomorrow and try to find out. Don't you worry Ami. We will do everything possible to find her.'

'Yes. Don't you worry Amidi,' Shruti said. 'Everything will be all right. Ma Durga will protect her. Don't you worry.'

Shruti put her arm around Amy again. Suddenly Amy broke down, tears flooded down her cheek, all her positive affirmations melted away in a torrent of salty downpour. Shruti drew her closer and held her as tightly as she could, Avinash too came near and put an arm around her sister. The two sat holding her till the torrent stopped... Suddenly Amy felt relaxed; a load had gone off her heart... She needed this. She needed to cry in the arms of her dear ones, the pent up emotion had become too much for her to bear... she needed a shoulder to cry upon which Soham could not give her. He was no less worried but his concern and anxieties under pressure of meeting professional deadlines had always resulted in high decibel blame games in which she was no less a participator and that didn't help things a bit, only adding more to her tension. Now in the company of these two she felt much more relaxed and secure, and hopeful that things would turn for the better... Twenty-six years have passed since she left this house but the bond hadn't slackened a bit. The concern in Avinash's voice was as much as her own and the warmth in Shruti's touch was genuine, something that she was missing all these years, and Oindrilla's sudden disappearance had made that sense of 'being alone' even more acute. Not that there were no friends and sympathizers and well-wishers there but they were not her own people and what difference one's own people can make she now realized sitting between these two.

A figure appeared at the door, a young girl smiling shy. Big dark eyes still fluffy freshly awakened from sleep.

'Your neice!' Shruti smiled.

Amy rose from her chair. She walked to the kitchen door and put her arms around the girl who was nearly the same height as her.

'So you are my dear Tania!' Amy held the girl in her arms and brought her into the kitchen. An inexplicable feeling of warmth surrounded her as she sat holding the niece close to her body looking at her fresh eager eyes. It was the same feeling of warmth she had felt so often holding Oindrilla close to her when she was younger and missed it later as her daughter grew up and the hugging and kissing dried its own natural course as with most Indian parents and their children, unlike their American counterparts who continue to hug and kiss till the end even if the warmth is long being replaced by cold indifference. Now her eyes were glistening with tears of joy as she basked in the warm nearness of her niece inspecting her features closely for the first time in her life. She felt perfectly at home.

CHAPTER
THREE

They came in droves as expected. The women of the neighbourhood, the boudis and the mashimas and the kakimas, most of them have grown old beyond recognition. There were new faces too, their daughters and daughter-in-laws and grandchildren. Questions were asked in predicted lines, and the answers were ready too - the conversation with Ganguli jethu really helped, now she could lie about her daughter without a flinch. What is your daughter doing now? Completed her graduation, taken up a job as a photographer with a publishing agency. Why didn't you bring her with you? She is busy with an assignment, had no time. Are you not looking for a husband for your daughter? No actually, she doesn't want to marry right now.

Shruti came to her rescue. 'Lunch is going to be ready soon. She will talk to you later' she said disappointing the neighbours who were forced to leave getting the signal.

Avinash's visit to the visa office did not yield any results. Kolkata acche Kolkatate (Kolkata has remained in Kolkata)- the old poet had written hundred years ago. How true even today! The festival season had begun so the clerks and officers had all gone in festive mood, the counters were empty and the phones went ringing, not before Friday when it all ended will they would be able to cooperate with the visitors.

'Don't you worry Amidi.' Shruti consoled, 'A delay of a few days won't matter. Please try not to think about it now and try to enjoy the Puja. Ma Durga will bring her back I am sure.'

The calm and confidence with which she uttered the words pacified Amy a lot. Did Shruti believe in what she said: 'Ma Durga will bring her back'? Belief worked she had heard so many times. But why could she never believe with confidence? It was not that she hadn't tried. So many times she had told herself, she would come back, she would surely come back... but every time doubt crept in before the belief solidified. She couldn't hold on to the affirmations... it was like trying to build a sand castle during a high tide. Every time the words tried to hold on to the belief, waves of doubt sprang from under and washed it away. There was a permanent hole in her mind, a hole through which doubt crept in a constant flow, diluting her beliefs, every resolution, every determination.

Someone was waiting at the door. The maid.

'Come in.' Amy called.

The girl entered smilingly, holding a broom in her hand. A young girl, hardly eighteen but married. The red sindoor sparkling between her hairs.

'What's your name?'

'Joytsna.' The girl answered.

'Where are you from?'

'Santoshpur.'

'I see. Is that your original home?'

The girl nodded in negative.

'Where is your original home then?'

'Bangladesh.'

Bangladesh. So she was one of those millions of unfortunates who had to leave their country of birth and migrate to another country in search of a better living.

'You are married. What does your husband do?' Amy asked.

'He pulls the van rickshaw.' The girl replied shyly.

'Do you have children?'

The girl smiled again.

'How many?'

'Three.'

Three! Amy looked at the girl with amazement. Such a young girl, not yet crossed her teens and already a mother of three! When did she get married then? Fourteen? Fifteen? She knew that poor people in this country always got married at an early age Even when she was here she had seen many poor girls who worked as maids in their neighborhood marrying under aged. Nothing had changed in all these years for the poor. They were still undernourished, still finding it difficult to make ends meet, still getting married young and producing numerous children. The change that had taken place was in the upper layer of the society – the creamy layer – the layer which she herself belonged. It was different in America where all strata of the society had benefitted from development. It was not that there was no poverty there but at least there was hope for all, which seemed to be absent here for a vast majority of the people.

The girl must have read the question in her mind. 'I got married when I was fourteen.' She said smiling.

Suddenly Amy felt terribly sorry for the girl. So young, yet mother of three. Must have left school long ago... Living as a refugee in a foreign land, traveling for hours in train to come to this city to work in houses, leaving the little children back home.

'Why are you standing? Sit.' She told the girl.

The girl smiled shyly again, and to her great surprise sat on the floor.

Amy was taken aback. 'Why did you sit on the floor!' She exclaimed, 'Sit on the sofa.'

The girl didn't respond, only smiled looking at her. Suddenly Amy remembered. In this land of hers maid servants never sat on the sofa or on the chair. They always sat on the floor. It was same decades ago when she was here. Her aunt would never allow any maid or any worker who would come to the house from outside to sit on the sofa. They had to sit on the floor. Their refreshments, normally tea with a couple of biscuits, were served on especially reserved cup and plates that too were placed before them on the floor. But if they were from the government department or practitioners of more respectable job the treatment was surely different. Peons and electricians and meter readers were not prevented from sitting on the sofa but a rickshaw puller or a drain cleaner were. And they were all comfortable with it. Every house in the city, the same practice was being followed. And it is being followed even to this day... Didn't anything change really then? Are all the changes cosmetic? Superficial? The basic human behaviours had remained the same, time had no effect on it. In America it was unthinkable. What would happen if she instructs the janitor to sit on the floor? Within hours she would be behind bars charged with the gravely serious crime of showing disrespect to a fellow citizen.

Looking at the girl sitting on the floor saddened her heart. She could force the girl to sit on the sofa for the time being, but did she have the courage to make it a rule? Did she have the guts to go to Shruti and tell her that from now on no one who visited this house should sit on the floor? No she didn't have the courage. This was no longer her own house, she herself was a visitor and she had no right to disturb the equilibrium that had been set. She was not a Gandhi, she was a very ordinary woman. In spite of her long years in America she was as ordinary, as meek and as poor as the one sitting before her on the floor. She might have changed but she was incapable of spreading the change among others. She might be the daughter of a revolutionary, but not a revolutionary herself and she had lost faith in revolution. Thousands of years of discrimination, thousands of years of injustice that had got into the blood flow of a nation that no revolution could change, no education could change, unless the wheel turned on its own in a great upheaval, no less bigger than a cosmic explosion. Even her father who was so well read and broad minded and had so vehemently spoken against oppression and social barriers, saw no discrimination in this practice inside his own house. Was it because he thought it was a custom to be observed, that's why he did not raise any voice? It was so unlikely of him. She still did not have any answers, her father was no longer with her.

Who were to be blamed for her father's death? Was it the movement, the failed movement that didn't bring the revolution it promised to bring, claiming only its worth by the bloods of hundreds of lives who had dared to believe in it? Everything was wrong – it was not the way it was supposed to be. Revolution could not come this way – her father said many times. The whole ideology it was based upon was manipulated by some people who thought violence was the only way. Everything seemed so hollow now, and so remote. Those blood curdling slogans 'Naxalbari Zindabad!', 'Charu Mazumdar Zindabad!' and the writings on the wall 'China's Chairman is our Chairman', 'The source of strength lies in the barrel of the pipe gun...' Young Calcutta in the early seventies was not questioning, but only dreaming, dreaming of a class free, oppression free world and later willing to shed blood – when everything began to fall apart... Bloods were shed indeed with tears of mothers and sons and sisters and daughters and nothing changed. The revolution never happened, the black marketeers and the hoarders and the landlords who were vowed to be eliminated didn't even flinch and carried on with their businesses and had gone global over time, floating public issues in the equity market; and thirty years later Che Guevara was nothing but a brand, an emblem liberally used to sell T-Shirts and music CDs. "What do they mean by 'Long live Revolution?" Soham once asked. "Doesn't that mean 'Long live oppression'? They want oppression to remain so that they can make revolution." It was a mockery, a pointed one and had to be ignored but indeed it is oppression that has 'long lived' as revolution lie dead and cold under the massive weight of the free market.

Amy heard the girl's voice.

'You have come from America?' The girl asked.

'Yes. You have heard of America?'

The girl burst out in laughter. 'Who hasn't heard of America? It's the richest country in the world.'

Really? 'What else do you know of America?' Amy asked again.

'America is imperialist. They want to destroy the third world.'

Amy's jaws dropped.

'Where - where did you learn all this?'

The girl smiled again. 'They say in party rallies.'

'Which party?' Amy knows but she wants to hear from the girl.

'CPM; Communist.'

'Oh, CPM.'

Amy knew that the communist party arranged rallies luring poor men and women like this girl with a paltry sum of money or the promise of a wholesome meal and made them chant slogans: 'Down with America! Down with Imperialism!' and slogans against the war in Iraq.

The American way of dealing with world problems had invited resentment in many parts of the world, the third world especially and this part of India had a long history of anti-Americanism. Even in her college days large rallies were taken out by students of her college and other colleges against the American involvement in Vietnam. She too had participated in a couple of such rallies with her friends, though not for ideological reasons. Her friends had urged and she couldn't say no. The same anti Americanism existed even today, only Iraq and Afghanistan had replaced Vietnam and those who participated in the rallies now were no more the Bengali intellectual class but poor men and women who understood nothing of the reason behind these rallies, they only knew America was evil – like this girl sitting before her.

Amy rose from the bed and lifting her suitcase on to the bed opened it. She felt the girl trying to get a glimpse of what lied inside. She took out sari from the suitcase. An old sari but as well as new, that she had worn only once or twice.

'Come here Jyotsna' She called the girl.

Joytsna came near, her eyes brightened up in anticipation.

'Here this is for you. Wear it during the puja.' Amy gave the sari to the girl.

The girl looked at the sari with disbelief.

'This must be very expensive,' she uttered.

'You will look very good in it.'

The girl looked at Amy, her eyes glistening.

'You are so good didimoni.' She said in a shaken voice. Then suddenly to show her gratitude and respect she lowered herself and touched Amy's feet with her right hand and then touched her own forehead. Amy was pleased.

47

'I have work to do. Will talk with you later didimoni.' The girl picked up the broom from the floor and clutching the sari close to her chest left the room.

Amy looked at the clock on the wall. It was eleven in the morning. Avinash had gone to office and Shruti was busy in household chores and her daughter had gone to a coaching class. Amy lay on her bed. The sumptuous aloo paratha the cook prepared for breakfast was still deposited in her belly making her lazy... She thought of Tania, the name was really interesting and very modern too.Though it has a Russian origin, it is very common as an English name too. Tania – meant 'Worthy of Praise.' She too had wanted to give her daughter an interesting name, she had thought of Anandita, meaning 'the one who brings happiness, having a similar ring to Amrita - her own name given by her father - meaning 'immortality' or the woman with holy nectar of life that maintains the distinctive partition between divinity and demonity. Its consumption would completely wipe off 'Fear' from one's mind which has been the root cause of destruction and extinction since evolution. The name changed to Amy permanently in less than a year of her arrival in America. She gave up in her effort of correcting people in her job all the time because it was too hard for Americans to pronounce. She was equally sad that the fatal mispronunciation had not only changed the name but also the meaning attached to it and she could not give her daughter the name she wished. Soham insisted that she should be called Ondria as that is a commonly known English name. As there was a lot of resistance from Amrita against it, Soham finally settled for Oindrilla because in both America and in India the meaning of the name was almost similar. Ondrea meant warrior and Oindrilla was the name of Lord Indra's wife who was also a great warrior. Amy too compromised in this situation so that atleast her daughter could have an Indian name. 'Why don't you change your name to Alex or something?' Oindrilla had often advised her dad as she wanted to fit completely in the American culture. Later of course she laughed whenever she was reminded of that juvenile suggestion of hers. She hated her name in particular often suggesting changing it to something Indian sounding but never having the courage to hurt her mother's sentiments... But her fascination with India ended there; all her other choices and likings had gone the other way despite Amy's efforts when she was younger. Grown up though she began to like Indian names though, finding them more interesting and experimental than the same boring and repetitive Stephanies and Mitchelles and Michaels - which according to her opinion hadn't changed since the days of the Saints - and not to mention Amys and Oindrillas.

Her cell was ringing, Amy picked it up lying in the bed. Soham. She had not called after giving him the news coming out of the hospital morgue. She was expecting him to call. But he didn't, maybe he was busy in some operation. Typical conversation, lots of advice on positive thinking... again... Amy listened more, spoke less and that too in monosyllables. It was not anger but surely some irritation; that a gulf had developed between the two since Oni had left could no longer be denied. She expected more from Soham, more than advices on positive thinking over the phone.

She felt relieved pressing the red button. Coldness had crept in much earlier, silently but surely taking the heat out of the relationship without their knowing, and now the warmth too. The exuberance of youth, the kissing and hugging had long stopped. All that had remained and would remain until one of them is gone was the sharing of the bed. The same bed, the same man who was now overwhelmed with his career and meetings, the same touch, but nothing was same anymore. Surely he too felt the same way. The same woman, the same body but the fizz had gone, never to return again. She was also to blame. Her obsession with her daughter - only now she acknowledged it was an obsession - had pushed everything else to secondary importance bringing more coldness into their relationship.

But things were different only a few years back. The three of them would sit on the big living room sofa watching a movie on TV after supper; it was always Oindrilla who decided which one to watch; Lion King, The Mummy, Stuart Little. And once in a month they would drive to Fun Republic in the evening on weekends, do some shopping before moving into one of the several auditoriums to watch the newly released blockbuster, again it was Oindrilla who decided, and then Oindrilla would ask for supper at McDonalds or KFC – but she would not let them enter any such fast food restaurants. Rice, chicken curry, dal –traditional Indian food she would cook for them after they went home. It would get late, Oindrilla would often fall asleep while eating, she had to feed her with own hands and then Soham would lift her in his arms and place her carefully on the bed so as not to wake her up. Then they would go into their room and turning the light off would undress. Surely no longer the adventurism of the youth existed, but still it was greatly satisfying.

Amy brushed aside the thoughts and rose from her bed. She still felt tired but sleep wouldn't come. Coming out of her room she roamed about the house. Coming down to the first floor she stood before a closed door. It was the room her aunt shared with her cousin sister Riya. It was not locked, a mild push would open it but Amy hesitated. Some closed doors made you nervous; not because you didn't know what you might find inside but because you knew what you would find inside and you were not sure about the effect it might have on you. Some closed chapters you were not confident of opening again, but open you must when you were so close. You want to get away from it by not remembering, but it catches you finally and engulfs you in its tentacles. That was why she was hesitating to enter this room. Amy pushed the door open and got inside. Riya was smiling at her from the photo frame hanging on the wall.. Amy sat on the bed and looked at the photo, tears flowed down her eyes. She always had the feeling that her aunt had loved her more than her own daughter and maybe Riya too had that same feeling so there was always a coldness that existed between the two of them; not rivalry, not hatred, but maybe a faint jealousy. Riya was jealous of the patronage she would get from her aunt - and no doubt she would get more - her aunt being more compassionate and forgiving to this motherless niece of hers while she herself was faintly jealous of her cousin sister's sexy looks and outgoing nature, and the attention that she would get from the boys of the neighborhood and later from the boys of the college they both attended. But again it was she who was better in studies and good looks all along, always getting higher grades right from the school days which might have added to the chasm. But now, looking at that smiling garlanded picture of her cousin sister, her heart broke in pain. She wanted to have a happy and a secured married life but was married to a guy who turned out to be an alcoholic. But Riya did not for once complain, only suffered in silence, the daily beatings from a drunken husband and abuse from a heartless mother in law, until it was too much for her to bear. She committed suicide by hanging herself. Aunt had fallen to bed after the incident and she blamed herself too for being in such hurry in marrying her daughter off. No amount of consolation from relatives even from her brother could provide any comfort. It took months for her to recover, but soon after those dark days swept over them. There are times when tragedies strike families like a cyclone that never seem to end and the members get stuck in it for what seemed forever. Fortunately she has escaped the tragedies, marrying a bright guy with a bright future and he took her in his wings and settled for a land thousands of miles away where promises of happiness beckoned. She did get happiness in that land at least in the initial years in spite of the struggles they had to go through together, though the anxiety and pain she had left behind in her homeland always remained with her.

She would suddenly get up from her sleep in the middle of the night because of some bad dreams and would think of her father and Riya, and aunt and Avinash and cry silently while her husband slept beside soundly.

Amy came out of the room and headed for the library. This was one place in the house where she had always found peace. Pushing the big wooden door she stepped in. Smell of old books hit her nostrils, Amy felt a surge of exhilaration within her. She stepped inside and closed the door behind her.

It had remained exactly as it was years ago. The rectangular room, three of the four walls covered with wooden shelves with glass doors, a large window on the fourth wall, draped in curtains. A big dark brown mahogany table and four straight back chairs stood at the corner near the window, the floor covered with dark red carpet. Amy came near the shelves and glanced around at the books that covered the shelves. Nothing has changed. Hard bound collections of Bengali literature-Tagore, Bibhutibhusan, Sharatchandra adorned the shelves to her right. The one to her left was full of English literature... Shakespeare, James Joyce, Virginia Woolf. The shelf to her left contained books on economics and Arts and philosophy and journals and periodicals. Amy opened the shelf and picked up a book from the upper rack. Principals of Macro Economics by Prof. Ardhendu Bose... She turned the pages. A sweet aroma emanated. She brought the book close to her nose and took a deep breath.

The clock ticked backwards.

CHAPTER
FOUR

Amrita folded the shirt carefully and kept it above the other three that she had already ironed and folded. She placed all four inside the suitcase beside an equal number of trousers. She had wanted to put another pair of shirt and trouser but her father did not want to take anymore.

'I will be there only for three days and will be going nowhere apart from the University. What is the use of so many clothes then?' The professor argued.

'But you would be meeting people Baba,' said Amrita, 'they might invite you to their homes. You can't give your lectures and visit someone's home wearing the same shirt.'

'No. No. Don't put any more,' the professor insisted, 'I want to travel light.'

'Who else would be coming to the seminar Baba?' Amrita asked.

'Amartya Sen and Bhagawati will come. And Galbreith too,'

'You mean P. Galbreith, the Nobel Lauriete!'

'Yes.'

'I wish I could go with you Baba!'

'I have no problem,' the professor smiled, 'I would rather love your company but your aunt, will she let you come with me?'

'No she won't!' Amrita sighed, 'She'll never let me travel so far. But I'd have loved to watch you deliver your speech in front of such distinguished delegates Baba!'

'You did see me giving speech once, didn't you?'

'Yes I did. But it was here only. And you didn't take me with you. I went on my own.'

She remembered the event vividly. It took place at her own college, at the Albert Hall. She bunked her practical class to attend the seminar, no passes were required for college students. The hall was packed with students from her college and other colleges in and around Calcutta. She was perhaps the only person present who had nothing to do with economics. She had come to watch her father only; he was one of the two speakers. He had spoken something on Market Equilibrium. She was not listening to what he was saying. Standing on one corner she was only watching him deliver the speech, and also watching the reaction of his words on the audience. There was spellbound silence in the hall and all eyes were fixed on him – as if a magician had cast a spell. Her father's baritone voice, his relaxed yet confident posture and the occasional movement of the arm had a captivating effect on the audience. She was indeed feeling very proud then. Baba had noticed her and a soft smile crossed his lips when their eyes met. Everything was going fine till someone from the audience shouted, 'You are a pimp of the bourgeoisie!' 'You are America's pimp!' A commotion broke out immediately, then a scuffle between the members of the audience. She saw her father leave the stage. She too left the hall.

Coming back home, she had asked him what it was all about.

'They wanted to shut me off, those radical leftists,' her father had explained, 'They wouldn't allow anyone who differ with their view to speak.'

'They were calling you America's pimp Baba!' That was one

allegation she had found very difficult to digest.

Her father had laughed. 'Anyone who does not tow the Soviet or Chinese line is America's pimp to them! Their class enemy! They had come not to listen to me and they would not listen to anything other than what they believed in. But when they saw the rest of the audience getting interested they started shouting. Typical fascist strategy, but these leftists have no problem making it their own. You know Ami when it comes to power play - the left and right – are all the same!'

'But don't they know that you are against the Vietnam War? You had been quite vocal about it.' She had asked.

'It doesn't matter to them whether I am against the war or not,' Baba had said, 'anyone saying anything in support of the free enterprise is a class enemy to them.'

That was about a year back. Things had deteriorated ever since. Her father had become more and more marginalized as Calcutta and Bengal moved more and more towards the radical left. A peasant movement that had originated in a village called Naxalbari in the northern part of the province, and its charismatic leader Charu Mazumdar had caught the imagination of a large section of educated middle class Bengali youth, for whom armed struggle was now the only means to bring equality among the impossibly unequal sections of the Indian society. The term 'Naxals' – used to classify these young men for whom the People's movement in China was the other great inspiration, and drew sympathy from a wide section of armchair leftists among the Calcutta intelligentsia, many of who were his father's friends and would often gather in the library of their house for a Sunday Morning adda or gossip. Mulling over the recent political developments while readily consuming the delicious refreshments that were prepared for them by the cook under aunt's supervision, they would vociferously put forward their almost unanimous left leaning point of views criticizing her father in the process – often quite uncharitably – forgetting that it was his food they were consuming.

His Baba however had stuck to his middle of the road approach, be it on economics or politics, convinced that there could be no radical solution to the nation's ills. To him democracy was a non-negotiable concept and no way could he lend his support to anything that involved transfer of power through non-democratic means. His firm belief in the 'mixed economy' theory that strikes a balance between the free enterprise and necessary government intervention also drew a lot of flak from his friends, besides friends who were turning into foes. Some of Baba's colleagues and students had abandoned the cozy comfort of drawing rooms and coffee shops and were now actively involved in the movement, fighting police and political adversaries in jungles and villages of rural Bengal and also in the urban jungle of Calcutta. There had been threats to his life and under pressure from aunt and well- wishers Baba had stopped expressing his views in public, no more writing articles in local newspapers, no more giving lectures in seminars held in the city's colleges and universities.

Amrita pressed down the suitcase lid and locked the latches.

'I hope they will not let interrupt you in Mumbai,' she said looking back up to her father.

'No, not there, I am sure about it,' the professor said smiling. 'The young generation in Mumbai are not bothered about revolutions and all that. They are more interested in setting up businesses rather than dreaming of a class free world.'

'There's nothing wrong in dreaming about a class free world.'

It was Avinash. He had just entered the room.

Before her father could say anything Amrita intervened.

'Please, please no arguments now,' she said raising her hands thus preventing nephew and uncle from entering into another round of debate. Avinash, like any other young college student of the time was greatly influenced by Fidel and Che and Mac and their struggles against the forces of capitalism and had often contradicted his uncle's liberal principles. The heated discussions between the two often raised the temperature in the house, but to the great relief of both his uncle and mother, Avinash was satisfied with his armchair status showing no intention of joining the movement that was going on, the movement that like a magnet had attracted and destroyed many a nubile minds like his.

'Shall I call a taxi? Or do you want me drive you to the station?' Avinash asked.

'Are you confident enough of negotiating Posta Bazar traffic?' The professor asked.

'You should have trusted me a bit more by now.' Avinash replied.

'O.k. Bring out the car then.' The professor smiled.

'I am going with you two.' Amrita said.

****

The train departed at the scheduled time. Seeing the professor off, Avinash and Amrita stopped by a tea stall at the platform.

The stall owner poured tea from a big steaming kettle into two small earthen cups. It was hot and some of the tea spilled over to Amrita's sari as she found it difficult to hold the cup that had no handle. She wrapped the end of her sari around the cup to lessen the heat on her hand.

It was extremely sugary and didn't taste good at all. Amrita made a face.

'Can't they make it better? How can one drink such a...' she lowered her voice so that the stall owner could not hear.

Avinash smirked, sipping into his cup, evidently enjoying his sister's dissatisfaction. It was he who insisted that they should have tea at the stall and that too in earthen cups instead of china ones – an effort to bring her sister down to the earth. Amrita had never liked eating or drinking at roadside food stalls or restaurants, partly because of her penchant for hygiene and partly because of the likeness of homemade food her aunt had grown unto her. It was not that she never had food outside.She had done that many a times with her college mates but never without some hesitation. Avinash knew it and did not spare the opportunity to tease his cousin.

'Does her highness want to have Darjeeling brew in a ten anna cup?' He asked chuckling.

Amrita heard the stall owner chuckling too. She looked away and gulped the rest of the tea at one go, and then threw the cup into the litterbin. Avinash lobbed his cup over to the train track.

Someone was tugging at her sari. Amrita looked. A little girl, dark and sickly, naked with only a cloth wrapped around her loin. She quickly opened her handbag, brought out a ten paisa coin and gave it to the girl careful not to touch the dirty hand. The girl went away smiling happily. Amrita felt relieved. But her respite was short-lived. Seconds after the girl went away another two kids – one boy and one girl – came running asking for alms. Amrita tried to shoo them away but they wouldn't go away. This time Avinash brought out his purse and gave the urchins a coin each. The two ran away beaming.

'Let's get out of here before more comes,' said Amrita. The cousins moved fast and were out of the station before more urchins and their older associates could mob them.

'You know what,' Avinash said once they were inside the car, 'sometimes I think Uncle is totally wrong when he says that nothing can be achieved by armed struggle. Twenty-five years of democracy, five general elections and what did we achieve? Only a three-fold increase in our population most of whom we cannot feed, cannot clothe!'

Amrita said nothing. She never liked to get into such futile debates. Armed struggle, revolution, class struggle... all these words had no meaning to her. Maybe it was her father's aversion towards the ultra-left ideology that had an influence upon her, or maybe it was just her lack of interest in politics. She had never dreamt of an ideal world like her cousin brother and many of her friends, her interests had been limited to her own subject, chemistry. The world of complex organic structures and chemical bonds had always fascinated her more than any political theories or rhetoric, be it left, right or centre. And of late her MSC final exams being over and her books temporarily shelved, it was the prospect of her marriage that had occupied more of her thoughts. She had never wanted to think about it more than her studies, but the world seemed to be conspiring in forcing her to think about it – the feminine world in particular. Wherever she went, neighbor's or relative's, the women would eventually zero in their conversations around her, her looks, her family pedigree and the potential she held for attracting a nice groom. And why, in spite of all that, her father was still not putting her up in the matrimony market. It was the same ranting she had to hear and bear at home from her aunt, though she knew too well why her brother was not at all enthusiastic in finding a match for her niece. He had done it before - for Riya - and had burnt his fingers at that. But her own daughter's misery had not deterred aunt a bit; once again she had begun a tirade, incessant and unavoidable.

She had tried her best not to get herself infected by the worries that all the womenfolk in the world were having about her, but could no longer steer clear off it; now she had come to terms with the inevitable reality – that her time had come. She had not discussed it with her Baba but she wished he did something, maybe not floating ad in the newspaper as he had done with Riya, but something else, some other avenues. As the days passed, and days into months, she could feel a tension building inside her, and with every marriage ceremony, that of her friends and college mates that she had to attend, she felt the tension mounting.

'You know Ami,' Avinash said shoving the ignition key into the hole, 'sometimes I feel I am being so selfish. So much is happening all around and I am just sitting in the sidelines and watching and debating and doing nothing.'

'That's because you don't have the guts,' Amrita said and immediately regretted what she said. Avinash went silent. Amrita cursed herself- an unpardonable slip of tongue. She didn't want to say it, it just came out. Nothing could be done now... She had hit right on the head, unintentionally yet lethally. Nothing could be more humiliating for a guy than being reminded of his lack of guts and that too by a girl, even if she is a sister. He was his brother, and they had always been frank with each other never being careful to care about each other's feelings, but never did she hit him like this before. Why didit come out, Amrita wondered. Was it because of his constant teasing that was becoming unbearable, a desire to hit back so hard that it ended once and for all? He had so often teased her for being an elitist like he had been only minutes before in the platform, in front of the tea peddler. She was a kind of Mary Antoinette in his eyes, living in her own crystal palace oblivious of what was happening on the ground. It was not true, she had often tried to argue, but that did not deter him from lampooning her, sometimes very unfairly. Yes it was true that there were times when she had herself unable to connect with many things happening around her, but she had never ever felt herself superior to others by virtue of her dignity. She had always maintained a distance but had never let others feel bad about it. She might have remained passive amidst all the ideological rhetoric in this highly charged political environment, but she was not out of sync with reality, she had her feet on the ground, though she was not obsessed about the firmness of her steps. She was surely not a Mary Antoinette. In spite of her aloofness she was very much aware of the gulf that existed, only she didn't have any urge to change things, she was satisfied with her own life, preoccupied with her own little joys and worries. The problem with Avinash was that like many of his peers he had this 'great urge' to change the world, but was not willing to abandon the comforts that he was used to from childhood. He was a mere dreamer, an armchair communist in its true sense, who'd rather theorize an armed struggle rather than taking up arms. He would argue vociferously, and make a caricature of others, and self-introspect, but behind all this theorizing and arguments and self-introspection was camouflaged a serious lack of courage that she knew too well but had never mentioned it... until now. A mistake on her part to mention the unmentionable, no mistake about it. She tried to think of something to say but could think of nothing.

'You're right,' it was Avinash who broke his silence, 'I don't have guts. I don't have the courage to bear the third degrees. A slap in my face and I would divulge everything to the police. I am a bloody coward.'

The two drove in silence. Amrita realized it would take some time to get things back to normal. She closed her eyes and tried to justify herself. What she said was right, Avinash deserved this. There was a big disconnect between the person he really was and the illusions he had filled his head with, he needed to be shown the mirror. She never had any illusions about herself. She had looked herself in the mirror and knew that she too was basically an ordinary woman with limited capabilities; just enough to care about herself and maybe her immediate near ones, but beyond that she was neither interested nor capable. She knew that she too was too weak to bear a police interrogation, unlike Pritha, her classmate at Presidency, who had not disclosed the names of her comrades even after days of savage torture by the police at the end of which she came out losing her ability to walk, and was now recovering at her parent's house in some distant village under the watchful eyes of the authorities.

She was not Pritha She was Amrita, an ordinary Calcutta girl, like million others, happy with her ordinary dreams and ordinary life. She wanted to complete her studies and do a job and get married. Rather get married first and then do a job with her husband's approval, so that her studies did not go waste. But whatever she did, she wanted peace. A happy peaceful life with a husband who would understand her, take care of her, and later bear a child or two- most ordinary aspirations of an ordinary Indian woman, yet so very fulfilling. That was all she wanted.

****

Amrita lay on her bed wide awake. Sleep wouldn't come now she knew. She had to remain awake till the wee hours, only then her eyelids would get heavy. This always happened if she was not in bed before twelve. She was not insomniac, but neither was she a sound sleeper either like Riya, who would be fast asleep within minutes of hitting the bed and would start snoring too, very lightly though - not the rumbling thunderstorm that came out of her mother sleeping beside her. She never admitted though that she snored even when Avinash taped it in his recorder and made her listen. The faint sound like a distant thunderstorm was almost inaudible beside the locomotive rumbling and hissing of her mother's. Riya never accepted that it was hers, but Amrita who was convinced had never let her sleep beside her. But they did share her room, especially during the exams when they would study together till late, sometimes till three, sometimes till four in the morning. Riya had humanities while she had science. She had always done her studies in silence while Riya had to utter everything aloud to remember things, even when she was in college. Her repetitive rigmarole of a single portion of a text in order to mug it irked her at times, especially when Riya would raise her pitch forgetting that there was another person studying in the room too, and she had to ask her cousin to quieten down. There had been many such small differences between them that had resulted in many a skirmish in their childhood; but as they grew up they learned to live with their differences. They were sisters and friends and shared saris and secrets between them, but despite twenty years of living under the same roof they could never become buddies. A chasm had always existed simultaneously with this coexistence, though it had never developed into rivalry at any stage, but neither did it go away.

When Riya left the house, she had felt a sense of freedom, a freedom from a constant feeling of being accompanied by someone. She enjoyed her new found solitude and she still did, but on nights like these when sleep wouldn't come and the solitude became too encompassing she felt the need of someone by her side.

Amrita never had any boyfriend, and unlike Riya had never responded to the guys who had shown interests on her. There had been many since the time she attained puberty. The looks that she inherited - more from her dad than her mom - were good enough to turn many a heads. Letters would flow in too, some posted, and some thrown from a distance but no one had the courage to approach her in person. Was it because of the dignified locks that people said she had, that held back the guys in some kind of awe? She had read the letters though, they were full of praises and requests to respond which she never did – either by a letter or by a smile. Not that she never wished to. There were a couple of occasions when her hormones rushed, and she had her crushes too. But she always had control over her heart and indeed her mind. Was it her natural instinct or something else? Why wasn't she able to respond? What prevented her? Was it her pride or Fear? Or was the yoke of her family reputation weighing down on her subconscious? Or was it a combination of all? Riya had none of these, she mingled with guys freely, breaking hearts and getting her heart broken in the process, crying and making people cry. She had felt vacant when she saw Riya skimming in love and sympathized with her when she was dumped. But when Riya dumped someone – and she did dump quite a few of her boyfriends as she got more and more experienced in the game of courtship – she abhorred her cousin for being heartless.

But Riya wouldn't accept she was being heartless.

'I respond to my heart as it makes me respond. When my heart beats I fall in love when it doesn't I come out. I don't hold back my heart like you.' That was how she responded.

But she used her mind too. She had fallen in love and came out of it, but never went ahead with any relationship to make it permanent. Either the guy didn't earn enough or his pedigree was not high enough to match her own. She had no problem at all to ask her mother to put her up in the matrimony market when she realized it was beyond her lone effort to get a good husband for herself. Her conscience was clear on this too.

'Marriage is too complex a matter to depend on the elements of the heart,' She had theorized, 'Many more things have to be taken into consideration especially in our middle class reality for a girl to get married. Security is the highest among priorities. Then there is caste. Love comes at the bottom.''But love should end up in marriage. That's its logical conclusion.' She had tried to argue.

'May be in Europe or America, where the society is not so divided up in class and caste and the pressure is not so overbearing as on us. But still how many white women marry black guys in America? How many fall in love in the first place? Even love is conditional my dear sister!' Riya had chuckled.

'Our Romidi married a lower caste guy, remember. And he wasn't rich either.' Amrita had given the example of Romidi, one of their distant relative who had shown the guts of marring a lower caste guy against the wish - and opposition - of the entire family.

'True.' Riya said, 'But is she happy today? She is not and you know it. She is castrated from the family and with two children and the husband not earning enough she is finding things very difficult to get going. I am sure she regrets her decision today. I am not going to regret my decision Amidi. I will marry someone who will give me security first. Love will come on its own. You may call me heartless but I am just being a realist.'

Yes, Riya was a realist all along. But luck was not on her side. All her calculations had gone wrong. And she blamed it all on her uncle who had refused to buy her a husband of her dreams. Amrita remembered everything. It was true that it was his father's firm insistence that no dowry of any form should be paid or taken by any member of the Bose family that had been responsible for a number of so called 'good' matches getting out of Riya's hand. She remembered the events vividly. An ad was placed in matrionial column of Sunday's Anandbazar – the Bengali daily with the largest circulation. Match wanted for Kayestha girl. 5'4, wheatish, good looking, good manners. Govt. service, doctor, engineer preferred. P. O. Box 3287. Letters came pouring in response to the ad generating a standard response thought up by Aunt and written by Baba. More exchanges of letters followed with the shortlisted few and then the visits began. The entourages consisting of the prospective grooms and their relatives and friends arrived on Sundays and they readily consumed the rasgullas and luchis placed before them on silver plates that auntie had brought out from the large iron trunk under her bed. And Riya had to appear before them dressed in her best saris, eyes lowered. She had to follow her mother's instructions to the letter; don't look into anybody's eyes, be polite, never speak on your own, speak only when asked questions. And many questions were asked. Do you know singing? What are the dishes you can cook? Do you know stitching? Of course the lads didn't ask the questions, most came from their mothers - the prospective mother in laws. Riya knew cooking all right, and she could sing too. She had a very good voice and could sing Rabindrasangeet, the songs of Tagore well. Her academic grades were not bad either, but she failed to pass the all important litmus test that all Indian girl had to go through: the test of the skin color. It was not easy to get the nod from the boy's family unless the girl had a fair skin, and some additional features that every Bengali male desired - big dark eyes and an oval face like a paan leaf. Riya did not exactly fulfill the criterions though she had reasonably good features, but her skin color proved to be a great disadvantage for her. Taking advantage of her shortcomings the demands for dowries were made – in cash and in kind – almost always disguised in the same humble request: we have no demands you know but of course you won't send your daughter empty handed...

A little enquiry and the mask would fall off: a pair of gold bangles and a necklace, a dining table and a fridge and twenty thousand cash – that's all what we need, and yes if possible a car... No! No! We are not talking of an Ambassador, a small Fiat would do, our lad is tired of going to office in crowded buses you know...

It was so disgusting to hear respectable men, rather women – the would be mom-in-laws in most cases – making such shameless 'requests'. But even more shameless was her boy, who would say nothing, only smile while his dad or mom spoke. Amrita wished her Baba to simply get up and show the visitors the door the moment such 'requests' were made, but she knew her Baba was never impulsive; he listened patiently and then in his usual unhurried manner - softly yet firmly - expressed his unwillingness to meet such demands. Amrita felt proud of her Baba on such occasions, but her aunt was not at all happy to see the visitors leave without any match being made for her daughter, and as one after another the 'visits' failed and time passed by, she voiced her opposition against her brother's 'high' principles.

'What's wrong in giving a bit of joutuk, it is not that we cannot afford to pay a little money. A dark girl like her, how can she possibly get a good guy if we don't pay a little bit for her?' Amrita often heard her aunt mutter under her breath, though never in front of her brother. Even Riya had begun to get resentful.

'I will never find a husband for myself' she once said to her one summer night while they were walking on the terrace together. Amrita felt bad for her cousin sister, but not for once did she doubt her father's resolution of not conceding to the unreasonable demands of the prospective would be's. She only prayed that a good match came up for Riya, someone who would not ask for any kind of dowry for her hand. It was not that no such proposal came, but they came from guys who failed to pass the basic criterion that was required to marry a girl from a respectable Bengali family: a decent permanent job with a decent salary.

'Isn't there a similarity here? Just as we are looking for a guy with a decent salary for Riya, the guys too are looking for a girl with a fair skin. And not finding it in Riya they were asking to fulfil the deficit with cash.' Avinash had made this observation during a conversation they were having in the library.

She and Baba were present and so was Uncle Roy, a good friend of Baba. He was a practicing barrister in the Calcutta High Court.

It was such an unexpected comment that all of them had gone

speechless for a while and looked at Avinash, totally stunned. Something like this coming from a guy who claimed himself to be progressive and was the editor of his college magazine was no less than a shocker. But again the agony of his sister might have forced him to take such a stance.

'Did I hear you right Avinash?' Baba asked without being able to hide the astonishment in his voice, 'Are you trying to justify the dowry system?'

'I have thought over it and have come to some conclusions.' Avinash said in a studious voice.

'May we know what is it?' Uncle Roy asked, 'It seems to me that you are trying to justify a tradition that had caused so much pain to so many people over ages... Do you know that in Bihar and U. P. there is a stipulated rate for grooms? A government officer groom had a price of fifty thousand while an IAS officer's rate is one hundred thousand! How do you suppose any girl's father could pay such a large amount of money? By selling his house? His land? Spending all his savings? It's nothing but a market out there! And you're trying to justify it?'

'Why does a girl wish to marry an IAS officer and not a clerk who works in some private company?' Avinash sounded aggressive while responding. Then he replied to his own question. 'Because the IAS guy earns more and would be able to give the girl a good life which the clerk with his paltry salary would never be able to give. And in return he wants a wife with a fair skin and good features. And if he doesn't get that in the girl, he wants cash instead. It's indeed a market out there, I agree. But yes, I do not support the exploitation that is carried out in the name of dowry. No one should squeeze anything out of anybody, that's inhuman. But if someone is able to pay...,' Avinash looked at his uncle, 'Then what's wrong in paying for a decent guy with a decent earning?'

Silence followed. Then Baba spoke.

'So you want us to pay dowry for Riya's marriage Avinash?' He asked.

'It's up to you uncle,' Avinash said, 'I have only voiced my opinion on this.'

Baba went quite. There was some logic in what Avinash said and it had driven home.

A rift had developed in the family, with she and her Baba on one side and the rest on the other, and it was painful for all of them. But then Baba did not have to compromise with his principles. Finally, not long after they had the conversation, a match came for Riya from an officer working with the Indian Railways and she got married. They did not ask for any kind of dowry and that was considered a great virtue by her academic uncle, but the guy to whom she got married had an even greater vice. He was an alcoholic and within days of her marriage Riya's life had become a living hell. She did not utter a word about her in law's, but the dark marks under her eyes and accounts of acquaintances from her in-law's neighborhood told the story. Riya's visits to her mother's house became less and less frequent, and now she had stopped coming altogether. Amrita knew that it was not her in-laws who were preventing her from coming home, but Riya's own resentment towards her uncle, who because of his high moral values had not let her marry some better guy who might have taken a bit of dowry that was not impossible for her family to pay, but in return had given her a better life. And that was what her mother – Amrita's aunt – thought too, though she never blamed her brother directly.

But her frequent sighs with the utterings, 'If Riya's dad had been alive the poor girl wouldn't have to see this day' made clear the resentment that she too had towards her brother's uncompromising attitude.

But her daughter's fate did not in any way lessen the love she had for her brother and his motherless daughter. Amrita had never felt any less love from her aunt than his own father; it was only their attitude towards things that were different. Her father had his education in London, and years of staying abroad had broadened his outlook towards life and society whereas her aunt's perspective was restricted to the confines of middle class Bengali parameters. But that had made her more pragmatic towards the reality of the ground and she was willing to make small compromises for the sake of her children, which her brother had found very difficult to. Notwithstanding the tragic outcome of her own daughter's marriage odyssey, she once again began to pester her brother to find a match for her niece. But this time Baba was non-committal. He had maintained a stoic silence whenever the issue came up. That had made her aunt jittery and she was losing her temper quite often over her inability to pressurize the 'once bitten twice shy' brother of hers, who was in no hurry this time. She had even threatened to go to the newspaper office herself and apply for the ad but even that had not moved the man. Unsuccessful though at her quest, she had been successful in implanting her worry into her niece's head who was now having sleepless nights, her mind just unable to stop the stream of same thoughts coming over again and again. There was no denying that there was a lot of sense in what Riya used to say and think. There were indeed some middle class Indian realities that a woman had to face, it was not easy for her to follow the heart and be happy at the same time. Was that the reason why she held back her own? Of fear of doing something that might cost her lifelong happiness? She knew unlike her cousin her conscience wouldn't allow her to pull out of a relationship without her soul getting bruised and so she didn't get into any relationship at all. She had held back her heart all along notwithstanding the futile beats within it, and the pangs of painful solitude and the bouts of jealousy she had watching her cousin bubbling in romance.

With Riya gone she no longer had to feel bad about her inability of her heart, but her loneliness was becoming too overbearing on her. For the first time it was not only pressure from the family and relatives that were making her think about her own marriage, but her own desire to settle down. If only she had been a little more adventurous, maybe not like Riya, but like her friends Sumita or Shimul, who had found partners for themselves right from the first year days without becoming a bother to their parents. She had remained trapped in her own mind and was now totally dependent on her father who would not disclose what was going on inside his mind, neither to his sister nor to his daughter, disturbing the peace of the family in the process.

Amrita heard the clock strike four times. The crows had begun to caw. In another half an hour the sky would begin to clear.

CHAPTER
FIVE

The professor looked at the faces around him, Amrita did not fail to notice the twinkle behind the spectacled eyes. She did not remember when was the last time they had all sat together around the table in the library. Aunt had never been present during the discussions and arguments they had here, and her presence in the library had always been brief, either to bring refreshments for the guests who came visiting regularly on weekends, or to instruct the maids to clean the dust off the shelves and over the books. But today, not even an hour had passed since he had returned from Mumbai, Baba had made all of them sit around the library table. He was going to say something important and the twinkle in his eyes said it was good news.

'I have met a boy,' the professor broke it finally, 'His name is Soham Ray.' The professor looked at Amrita.

Amrita's heart began racing. This was unexpected. She thought her Baba had a good offer somewhere.

'A very good boy ; Good looking,' the professor continued, 'Got a gold medal in MBBS and is working as a House Surgeon at Lilavati Hospital.'

'What does his father do?' Aunt asked. She too had sensed it right and came straight to the point.

'His father was a senior IAS Officer- Prashanta Bose, retired as Under Secretary of the Govt. of Maharastra. A very cultured family, and have a bungalow at Kalyani Nagar.'

'Siblings?'

'One brother, one sister. Sister is married to a Govt officer. Brother is younger, studying mechanical engineering.'

'Did you meet the father?' Aunt asked.

'No. I met the guy only. He came to my seminar. Can you imagine! A student of medicine attending lectures on economics! He met me after my lecture, we talked about macro-economics. He seemed to be quite informed! Knows a lot of things apart from his subject.'

'Did you tell her about our Ami?' The eagerness in aunt's voice was evident now.

'Oh, yes I did! He is not engaged, no girlfriends either. Looking for someone to settle down. He had agreed to come to Kolkata to have a look at Ami!'

'That's great!' Aunt couldn't hide her excitement.

'Get prepared girl!' Avinash chuckled thumping her back. 'Get prepared to charm the prince charming!'

Amrita got up from her chair.

'Aren't you interested?' Aunt looked up, startled.

'Won't you meet him?' The alarm in her father's voice was even more acute.

'I will.' Amrita said and walked away in quick steps.

'Shameful Diva!' She heard Avinash's comment as she crossed the door.

Back to her room Amrita sat on the edge of her bed looking at the checkered design of the floor under her feet. She could still feel her pulse throbbing, her mind was in a quandary. There was a certain no nonsense directness about the entire conversation that made her feel very uncomfortable. Baba shouldn't have initiated it in front of everybody. It would have been much better if he had discussed it separately with aunt and then with her; but he always had this 'no hush hush, open to all' attitude without caring a bit about feminine sensibilities... but what made her feel more uncomfortable was the fact that Baba had on his own initiated a matrionial dialogue with a complete stranger who was nearly half his age. That was degrading for a man of his stature, but the manner in which he was narrating it all clearly indicated that it didn't even occur to him that it was degrading, on the contrary he seemed to have felt rewarded, that such a good guy had agreed to see his daughter. God knows what else he had told that doctor to make him impressed about his daughter!

But at least he had broken the silence on the matter, at last! A silence that was so overbearing on her and aunt, at last he had set the ball rolling. Behind the stoic façade her father was worrying for her, perhaps more than anybody else, and now he was acting. Maybe not with the kind of guile that was required for such purpose but acting nevertheless, despite the hectic schedule of seminars and lectures... Poor Baba...

The metallic sound of keys colliding with each other told Amrita that Aunt had entered the room. She always had a bunch of keys tied at the end of her sari that dangled as she walked around the house, announcing her presence from a distance. And along with it the pungent sweet smell of Gopal brand zarda that she consumed with paan and broken beetle nuts, that could be smelled from a distance too.

The two sat in silence on the bed for sometime. Then aunt spoke.

'I hope this works out fine,' she said looking up to the framed photo of the goddess on the wall, staring at them with her bloody red tongue sticking out. 'I am sure Ma Kali won't let us down. You had kept fasts, you will get the result.'

Amrita did not fail to notice the sigh that her aunt tried to conceal. Riya never kept fasts in spite of her mother's insistence. She had no faith in rituals, had always rubbished the practice that all Hindu girls of marriageable age adhered to irrespective of class and creed, keeping fast on Mondays, pouring water on top of the penis shaped black stone that resembled Lord Shiva, the ultimate husband - of the tongue sticking goddess - whose tongue had come out in shame when she accidentally stepped over her sleeping hubby.

But she had listened to her aunt despite her ambiguous faith, obediently accompanied her to the temple on Mondays and had poured water on top of the shiny black penis stone that stood erect out of a concrete vagina shaped stone and like all other women had rubbed the slimy stone surface while pouring water or milk, as faithfully as she could.

'The boy will be coming next week. I will go to the Kalighat temple and offer prayers to the mother. I did not do it last time.'

This time aunt made no effort to conceal the pain in her voice. Amrita remained silent.

'I want you to look good. You can go to the parlor if you wish.' Aunt said caressing her long flowing hairs.

Amrita felt amused and bad at the same time. Aunt had always objected to their going to beauty parlors, never had faith in those 'strangely dressed Chinese girls' who applied 'what not's' on the faces of their customers. She had always preferred combing their hair with her own hands on occasions when they had to appear in public, and for special tips she would refer to her old book, the pages of which had turned yellow with time but still contained numerous valuable traditional Indian beauty tips, the ingredients of which she would personally fetch from the local market. But now she seemed to have lost her confidence, or was it her willingness?

'I am not going to go to any parlor,' Amrita said defiantly, 'I don't care whether he likes me or not.'

'Do what you think best! You are a grown up girl now.'

Aunt sighed once again, got up from the bed and left the room.

Amrita knew she had not told the truth. She definitely cared. She might have reservation on the manner in which Baba lured the guy, which seemed to be an act of desperation, but she had faith in her Baba's choice and she was not going to let this opportunity go out of her hand. She would do her best to impress the guy, if of course she found him impressive. She would indeed go to the parlor if aunt did not help, and she would put on the green and gold sari that she believed not only brought the best out of her but also brought her good luck.

****

A squarish face, clean shaved, with a strong jawline that radiated confidence, the eyes small yet bright behind a stylish expensive pair of glasses- that was was she observed when she looked at Sonam for the first time. The jacket seemed to be expensive too, maybe imported; it jelled perfectly with the fine nine, five ten sturdy built structure. No doubt impressive at the first look...far more impressive than his two friends who sat on either side of him on the sofa. The conversation they had so far was quite formal, and it was he and one of the friends who had spoken the most, apart from Baba of course. Despite the resolution that Amrita had made to herself that she would not remain shy and would participate equally in the conversation she found herself tight lipped, speaking only when spoken to. Avinash's presence would have helped her to relax, but despite his wishes to meet the prospective groom he could not stay over because of a competitive exam that he had to appear for.

But she could well see that her shyness had in no way dampened Soham's spirit who like his friends was finding it difficult to keep his eyes off her. That he had liked her was clearly evident from his smiling face and the eagerness in his eyes, even Baba had realized it. He was smiling too and talking, more than usual, unable to contain the happiness within him. She did not have to go to the beauty parlor, aunt had taken care of everything. That she had done a good job was obvious from the three pairs of transfixed eyes.

'Why don't you show Soham our library?' Baba said when it seemed the conversation had dried up a bit. Amrita realized that her father wanted the two of them to talk in private, otherwise he would have asked her to show all three of them the library. Or he would have taken them himself, a thing he loved to do when new visitors came to their house.

Amrita rose from the sofa, so did Soham, understanding the hint his two friends remained seated. One of them brought out a transistor radio from his trouser pocket.

'Won't you two come?' Amrita asked for courtsey's sake.

'You two go ahead, we'd rather listen to the commentary.' The guy holding the radio smiled and put on the radio.

'What's the score?' Amrita could not help asking. She was herself listening to the commentary of the India Pakistan Cricket match in her own room on the big Bush Radio before the visitors arrived.

The guy listened carefully holding up the radio to his ear.

'254 for 6. Gavasker and Solker batting.'

Amrita was relieved. Gavasker was still on the crease. As long as he was there India still had hope.

'You like listening to Cricket commentry?' Soham asked once they were in the library.

Amrita smiled and nodded.

'Had you ever been to a cricket ground?'

Amrita shook her head to say no.

'I never miss an opportunity to go to Brabourne stadium whenever England or Australia or Pakistan comes to Mumbai. I will take you with me when Australia comes in January.'

Amrita was startled and amused at the same time. They had not spoken more than a few words between them and he had not even bothered to know whether she liked him or not, but he spoke with such familiarity as if she had already become his wife... She liked it though. This cool confidence. She felt a surge of warmth inside her. A feeling of belonging bubbled within. She felt cozy in the company of this handsome young man.

'What else do you listen to?' Soham asked.

'Songs. Hindi movie songs, Bengali too. Chhaya Geet that comes on VividBharati at night.' Amrita said, no longer feeling shy.

'Don't you listen to westerns?'

Amrita shook her head to say no.

'I do. I like Frank Sinatra.'

Amrita tried to recall if she had heard of Frank Sian... No, she hadn't heard of any singer by that name. She had heard of Elvis Presley and Beatles – John Lenon – but never listened to them, only knew the names. But Frank Siantra? Is he English... She wanted to ask but didn't. It was better not to expose her ignorance at this early stage.

She wished Soham talked about Indian music, of Mohammed Rafi and Lata Mangeshkar and Kishore Kumar on whom she knew a lot more about.

Lucky for her, Soham was more fascinated by the collection of books, and their conversation revolved around the books and authors. Though not a book worm in the true sense of the word, she was not averse to reading, and unlike her cousin sister had not restricted herself to text books only. Amrita talked confidently about Dickens and Tolstoy, and Hemmingway – her favorite. But she was careful to steer away from Virginia Woolf and Dostoevsky that adorned the shelves but that had gone over her head every time she tried to get a hold on them. Soham candidly admitted that he hadn't read much of Bengali literature and had no intention of doing so. That saddened Amrita a little, she had read more Bengali literature than English. It would definitely be great to have a husband who'd have appreciated Tagore and Bibhutibhusan. But you can't get everything...

But she was soon to learn that she wouldn't get a few more things. As the conversation veered into their respective subjects and she told Soham her intention to do her Masters in Radiology and later take up a job in a hospital, he went quiet for a moment.

'I am not sure if you will be able to do a job. ' He said finally, again confidently assuming that she had already become his better half.

'You don't like women working?' Amrita asked, carefully avoiding mentioning 'me' or 'your wife'. Though she knew well that she would no way reject this young doctor, her feminine instinct did not allow her to sound as familiar as him.

'I have no problem at all!' Soham exclaimed, 'In fact I'd appreciate if you work. But...'

'But what?'

'No woman in our family ever worked. Neither my mom, nor my sister.'

'Would they mind if I work?' Amrita gave up her pretence and began talking in first person.

'They might, my mother in particular. But I have no problem!' He said again, 'If you are hell bent in doing job I will support you at that.'

Amrita was pleased to hear that, but a shadow of concern crept into her mind about her would be in laws, the mother in law in particular. What kind of person would she turn out to be? From what she had heard from Baba and from what she had seen of Soham so far it seemed they were a different family from her's – more anglicized than traditional, why this mental block about women doing job then? Was there an element of hypocrisy there?

Amrita brushed aside the thought. He was o.k. No hypocrisy in him, she was sure of that. And that was what mattered most. He was better than she had expected. Sauve, intelligent, with a sense of humor. And good looking. What more she could have asked for? Getting married and settling down was her first priority. Job would come later. She wouldn't go for a job at the cost of her mental peace, or that of her husband or that of new family, if it came to that.

'My friends would be leaving tomorrow.' Soham said, 'I plan to stay over for a day or two. I'd like to get a feel of the city, would you help me at that? I haven't been here since I was a boy.'

'Sure I would!' Amrita said, elated at the prospect.

'Which is the one place in Calcutta you would like to show me? If in Mumbai I would take you to Colaba, that's the most interesting place in the city. Gateway of India, Taj Hotel, Appollo Bunder – the Arabian Sea...'

Amrita didn't have to think twice. She knew where she would take

Soham. The place where he would get a real feel of Calcutta, a place she knew like the back of her hand: the street where her college was – College Street. No sea there, no monuments, no big hotels only a narrow street with tram lines engraved upon, lined by innumerable shops on both the pavements that made walking difficult, all stuffed with books - all kinds of books – new and old, glossy, fresh out of print to worn out coverless second-hands, from nursery rhymes to research materials and rare books – everything that had ever been printed. Behind the stalls lay hidden the institutions - colleges and schools - hundreds of years old, among them standing apart in its grand magnificence is the Presidency College – her own college, the oldest and the most respected in the whole country. She had no doubt Soham would like it all; the smell of books, the flow of humanity - students, from tiny to old, academics, readers, writers, laymen, radicals and nothing-to-with's - all mingling together, walking the pavements, coming in and out of the schools and colleges and the university. Then there is the Coffee House which was a culmination of all – the two floors and the balconies crowded with students and professors and poets and writers and political activists all engaged in some kind of discussions, and laughter over a joke, chorus songs painting a red, class free, oppression free world, and furious high decibel debates over communism and capitalism and all other isms that had ever been formulated... and in some corner a couple quietly exchanging love vibes over a cup of two rupee coffee for hours, a poetry book open on the table between them, their soft murmurs of affection lost in the din. Every time she had sat around the tables with her college mates her eyes had looked for such couples and every time she wished she too had someone... someone with whom she could talk for hours holding hands over a cup of coffee, dark and steaming, looking into his eyes, weaving dreams... She'd do it with Soham. They would share a table between them, the coffee would be of Soham's choice, they would know more about each other chatting amidst the din, lost in the crowd.

There might not be love yet, but they would share the affection that had already grown between them, bask in its warm nearness, building foundation for the bond that would see them through the journey they would be taking together...

'What are you thinking?' She heard Soham asking.

'Oh nothing!' Amrita came out of the stupor, reddening a bit. I'll take you to a very interesting place.'

'What is it?' Soham asked.

'Let it be a secret for the time being.' Amrita smiled mysteriously.

CHAPTER
S   I   X

It was the most exciting wait of her life...

Innumerable times over the years she had waited sleepless, for the night to pass over, bearing a heaviness in her heart in anticipation of the day that would follow, the day the result would be out and she would know her grades, the percentages, or whether she had cleared the hurdle she had tried so hard to. Then there were the waits in the doctor's chambers in overwhelming fear, pulse running fast for the needle to be pushed into the arm or into the gums of the teeth. And the long wait, dry and empty, spanning over God knows how many years in solitude of her own - for the man in her life; the wait that had ended finally with Soham appearing on her horizon.

Now she was waiting for him again in a blood warming, heart throbbing, fear rousing anticipation sitting in a large bed adorned with flowers. In a few moments Soham would step into the room pushing open the door and then closing it again... for the first time in her life she would be alone in a room with a man behind closed doors, over a white bed sprinkled with white flowers that had not turned red yet.

Her friends were rather charitable in offering her their advices for this occasion. They had all come, Tinni, Shimul, Tina, Rashmi – all married and experienced and the few who were yet to sit on the piri, Preeti and Sonia among them. All her cousins had come too, and all her aunts from far and near, from both her mother's side and her father's side and for the last two days she was under their custody; only Riya hadn't come despite her repeated requests over the phone. She was woken up early in the morning the day before and made to eat puffed rice, curd, sweets and jaggery – the only meal she had during the day till the entire ceremony was over, and was then bathed in pre collected rain water that washed away the turmeric paste that was being applied on her arms and face. She was dressed up in a new Benarasi sari that she and aunt had bought after scouting half a dozen sari shops in Gariahat Market causing the shopkeepers shuffle in unspoken irritation, and under her watchful eyes the women decorated her with great care like a mannequin in a showroom; they washed her, brushed her, powdered her and groomed her, and cajoled her all the while with feminine praises, advises and jokes - erotic at times when aunt was not present - causing flurries of laughter. Sandalwood paste was used to draw small semi lunar shaped designs on her forehead, her hairs were wrapped up in a bun held together with a bunch of pins, gold bangles were glided through her wrists and a pair of conch shell ones, to be worn with pride all through her married life, and to be broken in tears if it ended in her husband's death. A heavy diamond studded gold necklace that made quite a dent in her father's bank balance, that she wanted to be replaced by a cheaper one but her aunt insisted upon, was hung over her neck. All throughout the day gifts were exchanged between the two families. Soham's parents and sisters had come from Mumbai along with a few relatives and friends. They had rented this house in New Alipore, the poshest locality of the city from where they carried out the customs that were required for the groom's family to adhere. Large straw plates containing sweets, saris, fish and cosmetics wrapped up in yellow cellophane were sent on his parents' behalf, and from her side similar presents packed in similar fashion were sent back to them, only instead of saris a set of Dhuti Punjabi and male cosmetics were packed for the groom.

The groom party arrived in the evening. A triangular, front only thermocol crown mukut was placed upon her head tied at the back by a string. Soham too was made to wear a thermocol pyramid shaped hat that rose a feet above his head; with this topor on his head and wearing the Dhuti and Punjabi and a white flower garland hanging over his neck he looked as funny as any other Bengali groom despite his handsome features. He was made to stand in the middle while Avinash and her other cousins lifted the wooden piri she was sitting upon cross legged and made her circle around Soham seven times amidst the ululate from the women folk, she had covered her face with a paan leaf that blocked her from looking into the groom's eyes. She removed it when told to after making the seven circles, and their eyes met amidst a fresh round ululation, claps and laughter. Then they both sat cross legged on either side of a square, brick lined pit on which the holy flame burned, flaring up every time the priest sitting between them threw ghee and sulphur into it, chanting mantras in Sanskrit all the while that she and Soham had to repeat and so was her Baba who sat beside her. Under the priest's instruction Baba held her hand and placed it over Soham's, she was being handed over to her husband. His dad and mom and sisters and other relatives stood watching behind him. It was unusual for the groom's mother to be present at her son's wedding, but her mother - in - law had broken the rules giving her the first hint of what kind person she was. They stood up, the priest tied the end of her sari to that of his dhoti and she followed him in circle, this time on feet round the fire. Seven times once again, as the onlookers counted the rounds at the end of which she officially became the wife of Soham Ray.

She was feeling pretty tired by then and hungry too. The two sat together and ate from the same plate being forced by public demand to put rice into each other's mouth. The groom party had left by then and she and Soham were at the mercy of the women of her faction. They made both of them sit together on the mattress in the basar room and throughout the night games were played and songs were sung and jokes flew abound. She was worried that Soham might lose patience as she herself was getting irritated, her fatigue getting the better of her. But Soham, despite the often boring and often juvenile overtures from the girls, seemed to be enjoying the company, basking like a prince charming amidst the feminine cacophony.

By dawn the girls were all asleep on the mattress and she too, reclining on Soham's chest. A car was ready to take them to her in-laws rented house. Somewhat to her relief, and a bit to her surprise and concern, she discovered the absence of rituals in her new family, all she had to do was bending over and touch the feet of the elders of the family and giving each of them a sari or a dhuti. She noticed her mother - in - law dragging her feet not letting her touch her feet though she embraced her warmly and planted a kiss on her forehead. A small silver box was handed to Soham, he brought out a pinch of vermillion sindoor and dashed it midway over the lane that ran through her parted hair, another symbol she had to wear all through her married life.

Come evening a reception was held at the hall, she had to sit on a sofa with Soham beside her, smiling mechanically at the guests – most of whom were from her side. Soham whispered to her ears that another reception were to be held once they were in Mumbai, it would be on a much grander scale at the lawns of the Mumbai Gymkhana. A slight flutter went through her stomach hearing Gymkhana, were it not the place where the who's who of the society gather and made merry over bouts of whiskeys and champagnes? She looked at Soham. No doubt he drank too. But how much?

The door opened. Soham. Amrita's heart began to pound like never before. She couldn't look up straight at him, into his eyes as she felt a desire unknown before surge through her body. Inexperience shot panic alarms all throughout her nerves and brain, not knowing what to expect, while her heart longed to be in the arms of Soham wanting to feel assured by this man, in a completely new and unknown relationship to be explored together, amidst a completely unknown bunch of people who were now her new family, each having their own set of expectations. Soham met her expectations with confidence. He held her hand in a warm grip and took her to the beautiful bed adorned lightly with flowers and made her sit on it. Her brain pumped an extra surge of adrenalin and her heart thumped wildly when she remembered all the scenes in Bengali and Hindi movies that she and Riya had seen together of this special onetime moment in a couple's life as they all say. How and what will be their's like?

"Well? Did you enjoy your gala day?" Soham asked. Ami was instantly startled by this question as she least expected this now but was she immediately warmed up towards Soham finding a new friend in him.

She immediately responded, "I did, though it seemed never ending at times. Did you?"

Soham responded with a warm smile immediately acknowledging their need to get rest now and explore this newly won relationship. "Let's get some rest now" he said; "Let's get ourselves back in something lighter before we call it a day. I'll help you , as you have more things to take off your body than me". Soham had an impish grin on his face as he started working on unwinding the diamond necklace from Amrita's neck, and unashamedly she admitted to herself that she liked the way he initiated the course of the rest of the night. In no time, wild fire razed through her body and engulfed her being...the feeling of being possessed by him- her man!

****

Next morning they were in a cab once again, heading towards her Baper Bari – her father's house, which had been her house only a day before but no longer. From now, she was a member of her Sasur Bari - her father-in-law's house. Soham need not have to have a Baper Bari though, even if he shifted to a house of his own, no Indian male had a Baper Bari where they returned to, only the women did. They were to stay there for another couple of days – again a ritualistic requirement – then head for Mumbai where her Sasur Bari actually was.

It was quieter than she had expected. The relatives had not left yet, they were to stay over for a day or two more, especially those who lived far away... but no hustle bustle could be heard. No women voice shrilling out, no child crying... The door did not open automatically as she had expected. The driver had to honk the horn a few times to make them aware of the presence of the newly weds. But still the door remained closed, and no one came out to welcome them. Amrita felt embarrassed and irritated. What would Soham think? She thought of getting out of the cab and knocking the door herself when it opened. Shubho Kakima, was standing at the threshold. Amrita and Soham got down from the cab and climbed the steps. Amrita lowered herself and touched Shubho Kakima's feet. She felt her hand over her head. Straightening up she looked at kakima's face, no smile in it. Kakima's face was grim, eyes glistening.

'What happened!' Amrita asked.

Kakima averted her eyes, Amrita looked sideways. They were all standing in the hall, immobile in their respective positions. Baba, Aunt , Avinash, her other aunts, uncles, the children... all silent...

'What happened!' This time Amrita let out a shrill.

She saw her aunt collapsing to the floor, crying uncontrollably. Baba came forward and drew her into his arms. Avinash wrapped his hand around Soham's shoulder.

'What happened!' Amrita whispered, looking up at her Baba's face.

The professor held her daughter tightly as tightly as possible.

'Riya hung herself last night.' His voice was barely audible.

****

Through the faint blue darkness of the cabin Amrita looked at the dark figures sleeping on the bunks opposite hers. The one at the lower berth snoring lightly under the blanket was her mother-in-law and the one above her also wrapped in blanket and emitting intermittent thunders, was Soham's father. In the dark of the confinement, stripped of the sophistication they wore in their awakened state, they looked so remote, so faraway amidst the constant jerk of the coach and the friction of the rails... Soham was in the bunk just above her, sleeping dead silent without making a sound. Was he there? Amrita wondered. Or was it somebody else? Were those on the bunks her own, or were they strangers who would get down at some station on the way, leaving her alone, helpless, in the dark?

Riya was alone, all alone in a city of millions, no one reached out to her... she couldn't come back. She never came back... she called her, pleaded her to come, over the phone, but she didn't. Had she made up her mind by then? She would never know, never know.

The train was slowing down. Is it a station approaching?

Amrita raised herself up and looked out of the glass window. The train was rolling into a dark platform. It was eerily quiet. No hustle bustle, no travelers waiting, no porters, no one getting down; only a few dark shadows, head to foot covered, sleeping on the benches and on the floor. A lone voice at a distance calling out 'Chai', a dog barking... What station is it? Amrita tried to look for a signboard. But she couldn't find one. All she could see in the blue darkness was a shed at a distance, and a yellow signal far away. The train stopped briefly then kept rolling, past the benches and posts, the little boy still shouting 'Chai', a half lit room, a man waving a green lantern... a sign board... Amrita tried to read, but couldn't... the train had picked up speed again.

CHAPTER
S E V E N

It had been a day like no other. For the first time in her life she had stepped into a cricket ground and watched the game. The men in white, whom she had only imagined in the expanse of her mind pressing her ear to the radio, listening to the commentary on medium wave, had suddenly appeared real before her eyes. Dennis Lilie, running like an express towards the twenty-two yards, delivering the ball then with a smooth swing of the arm, Gavasker standing at the other end stepped back a little and swerved his bat, sending the ball to the boundary line with a perfect square cut. The stadium erupted in a thunderous applause; she too had clapped like a little girl sitting beside an ecstatic Soham... It was dream come true. While in Calcutta she had so wished to go to the Eden Gardens to watch a match like this, but like so many of her other little aspirations that too had remained unfulfilled. Today her dream was realized.

Now sitting beside her husband at the embankment, looking at the orange sun immersing itself into the waters of the Arabian Sea, the dark gray waters splashing her naked feet, she didn't want to go back to the house that was supposed to be her home. It had been six months that she had left her father's house, a long six months that seemed no less than six years. She had not been able to adapt to her new environment, in spite of her best efforts, in spite of Soham's best efforts to help her out. She felt like a fish out of water, a total misfit. She knew it would be different, but so different she could never have imagined. The reception at the Mumbai Gymkhana that was arranged soon after their arrival at the city by Rajdhani Express – her first ever train travel in first class – was an eye opener. But it was the house of her in-laws that was the first shocker. Never before she had stepped into such a grand mansion in her life; she had seen it only in movies. A chauffer dressed in impeccable white was waiting for them at the Victoria Terminus in an equally dazzling white Chrysler that was air-conditioned. Again a first for her. They traveled through the city to Malabar Hill. Despite her wishes she was not able to enjoy her first view of the city. She had fallen asleep, the previous night's sleepless fatigue had got the better of her. A nudge from Soham, made her open her eyes to find the car rolling past a high iron gate along a concrete driveway flanked by flowered gardens towards a white double storey gothic villa. Her heart began to thump against her chest, it had not stopped thumping since. The inside was even more fascinating. Marbles, chandeliers, paintings, vases, mahogany strewn across the rooms in plentiful, fascinating, captivating, yet painfully alien... it took quite a while for her to reconcile to the new surroundings, she was not sure if she had reconciled fully even today... If the marbles and vases and the paintings were alien, the people and their ways were foreign, English to be precise. She got the first feel at the reception that was held in her honor at the Mumbai Gymkhana which was not very far from where they were sitting now. In fact it was in the morning that day when Soham's mother called her to a room fitted with a large mirror that she really began to understand it all. A lady was waiting, with a box by her side. Soham's mother said she was to cut off her long hair short. She was horrified to the point of running out of the room.

'Why?' She had asked in stupefied amazement.

'You will look good in a stepped cut.' Her mother-in-law said with a slight smile. The hair dresser nodded in agreement.

'Sit on the stool.' She heard her mother-in-law saying.

For a second she thought of doing as told. But then, looking at her reflection on the mirror, her long hairs flowing down on either side nearly up to the waist, she thought of the winter afternoons that were spent sitting over a straw mattress on the terrace of their Gariahat house under a soft cozy sun with her aunt combing their flowing hairs with great care - hers and Riya's - while the two of them read from the text books open before them, she in silence, Riya in a low murmur, simultaneously peeling oranges off the skin, chewing the koyas, spitting out the seeds.

'No, I won't cut my hairs.' She said softly but firmly looking down to the floor, then deliberately lifted her eyes and looked straight into her mother-in-law.

She remained silent for a moment; then instructing the beautician to do the grooming without the cut she left the room. Amrita realized that she had dropped the gauntlet; the battle of nerves had begun. She did wear a gown though at the reception, that her mother-in-law had chosen for her. But not the high-heel shoes for fear of falling.

It was something she never thought she would experience in her life. She felt she had stepped into one of such scenes in the Hollywood movies she had watched in New Empire and Lighthouse. Men, all in suits with bows fitted at the collars smoking pipes and cigars, women dressed in gowns that were without sleeves and backs, skirts that rose above the knees. The few who had come wearing Indian outfits wore blouses that were equally revealing, that she had only seen the actresses wearing in the pages of Anandlok. But what shocked her most was the fact that all were drinking, even the women including Soham's mother and sister. She was offered drink too by the orderlies, but Soham responding to her helpless look cleverly substituted the hard liquid with soft, all through the party she sipped Thums Up that looked no different from the whiskeys and Scotchs on the other glasses. The visitors were extremely courteous and well behaved though – initially at least – greeting her with flower bouquets. Only flower bouquets though, nothing else, and that disappointed her a bit. In Calcutta she had received so many varied kind of gifts from her own acquaintances: from saris to ornaments to books to utensils, none of which she could bring with her. She had to talk in English with everybody and she thanked her Baba for that, for sending her to Lady Brabourne instead of any Bengali medium school.

As the evening proceeded, music and wine flowed freely, the men and the women danced together, changing partners just like she had seen in movies. A few men came to her and asked her to dance with them. She dreaded every time, looking up to Soham who skillfully managed to ward off the suitors. The dancing got more and more wild and hysteric as the hours passed, and the masks of sophistication started wearing off. Men shouted, women laughed falling over the men. Suddenly the novelty factor that had kept her attracted to the show was gone, she wanted to quit. Soham brought her home much before it all ended. Much later, the clock striking three, she heard her in-laws returning; their high pitched, drunk voices could be heard from her room. She had panicked then, looking at her sleeping husband, wondering how he would be able to protect her from them.

Later though her fears subsided, she soon realized that her in-laws were perfectly normal human beings with perfectly normal human emotions, only the expressions of it were in a different plane that contradicted greatly with the traditional Bengali values she was brought up with. The sophistication of her family sprang from a deep rooted bondage with the Bengali culture that had imbibed English thinking without uprooting the core Bengali values, while

Soham's family had done away with the Bengali roots – altogether, except for the total abandonment of the language that they still spoke, in between their flawless English.   But sometimes she wondered how much of this modernity was for real and how much superficial. Despite their degrees in English literature, despite the wines – to her great relief she found that they never drank at home, only served to guests – the outfits, haircuts, the discussions on world politics, arts, Beethoven and Mozzart the women in the house could never think of going out and doing a job, and neither could get over the temptation of waving the stick over the daughter-in-law. Her father, on the other hand, despite preferring to wear dhuti punjabi over suits and trousers all his life had always wanted her to take up a job after completing her studies. 'Every women should be financially independent' he had so often said. It was she who had given marriage preference over anything else. Did she regret it now?

No she didn't. She had Soham and he was a league apart from the rest. It was indeed surprising to her, how could her husband develop an attitude that was so different from her parents and siblings. Soham had explained. He was the only among the siblings who had all his schooling in boarding schools away from home, where he had to do everything himself, from washing to cleaning, and mingling with boys from different backgrounds. His circle of friends got even bigger when he entered college, where students from poor families got admission too because of their merit; mingling with them and the patients who came from even more diverse background had dissipated whatever class barrier he had in his mind. It was true. She had found Soham even more flexible and adjusting than her. He had no problem in chatting with the waiter over the cricket match while they were having lunch at the stadium cafeteria, and now it was he who insisted that they should sit at the embankment in front of the Gateway of India to get a better view of the sunset.

The sun had set. The orange had turned purple. The birds that were circling above were no longer there. All gone home. Amrita looked at her watch. Quarter to six. It's time for them to return too, to a place she did not want to call home. But return she had to, before it was seven. To attend yet another of the endless parties where she had to smile, talk, walk around shaking hands, mechanically, without any desire of doing so. She wanted to get away from it all- back to her father's place, amongst her own. It had been six months, six long months.

'I did not tell you,' Soham said once they were in the cab, 'I am planning to migrate to U.K.'

Amrita looked at Soham with amazement.

'Migrate?'

Soham nodded. 'Don't you want to settle in U.K.?'

Her first impulse was to say no. Migrating to a foreign land was an impossible thought, it had never crossed her mind. She just wanted to get away from the house she presently lived, to get away from the people who lived in it. She had thought of telling Soham to find a rented house somewhere else, where only the two of them could stay. But she knew it would be impossible for him, not only because of the attachment he had with his family despite the differences, but also because of the family reputation that could not be compromised with. They could shift to some other city of course, Soham could easily get a job in Calcutta hospital if he wished, or set up a practice...

'I don't want to stay in this country anymore. I want to leave this city. I can't take this anymore!' Soham said without waiting for her response.

'Can't we move to some other place? Mumbai... Kolkata?'

'No. I don't want my parents to feel that I am getting away from them because of you.'

Amrita preferred to remain quiet. She knew well that it was getting too much for Soham to bear. This cold, silent, yet stressful battle she was fighting with her in-laws, on a daily basis. He had tried but failed to build a bridge.

'But is it right time to go to U.K.?' She remembered reading an article in Times of India about the current situation in Britain. It didn't seem conducive for migrants, especially those from the subcontinent. The present Government under hardliner Enoch Powell was discouraging Indians, Pakistanis, Bangladeshis to come to that country.

'You are right,' Soham agreed, 'they are driving out Indians from U.K. Kenyans o.k, but Indians no.'

'Why go to a country where we are not welcome.'

Soham nodded in agreement.

'It's not that I haven't thought of it Ami. It won't be prudent to go there now. And you are right. Why go to a country where Indians are not welcome... But I will leave India for sure. I will apply for U.S. visa then. Everybody is welcome there.'

Amrita looked out of the window. From the heights of Malabar Hill the lights of Marine Drive looked like a garland hanging in the dark. 'Queeen's necklace' they call it. Which queen? Victoria? Elizabeth? First or Second? No queens in America. No kings. Only Presidents. The all- powerful President of the most powerful nation on Earth.

'What do you say?' She heard Soham asking.

'You have already decided.' Amrita replied.

****

Her mother-in-law was discussing fashion accessories with the guests, and her father-in-law was lecturing about the present political situation in Bengal - his pet subject for the past few weeks. He tried to involve them in the discussion but Soham skillfully got away, as he always did. He always had the excuse of getting back to his studies, she had none. She had to sit through it in stupefied boredom, the same discussions over and over again; they never seemed to get enough of it. America wouldn't be a bad choice after all. She was prepared to go even to Timbuktu given a choice, to escape this daily dose of intellectual injection. She thought of going to the kitchen to assist the cooks. Her mother-in-law wouldn't object to that. This was another irony. The sauve lady rarely entered the kitchen and her daughter never; but they had no problem in sending the daughter-in-law. English culture rather Indianised here! She abhorred it initially, but now she found the kitchen more comforting than the sunroom – at least no superficiality here. She could talk in her mother tongue with the Bengali cook without having to switch over to English. But again she had to be careful not to sound too familiar, class dignity had to be maintained. Even Soham maintained the decorum while at home. Poor chap! Caught between family reputation and natural instinct! And on top of that, the wife. Better if he migrated.

The guests left late. They praised the cook for the mutton curry who in turn diverted the praise to her. She did nothing though, only gave a couple of tips her aunt had passed on to her. Nevertheless she basked in a flurry of praise, a rarity for her in this house, she felt her spirit invigorated. Getting back to her room she found Soham at his desk studying. She thought of taking away the books from him. It had been a good day today. They watched a cricket match together, enjoyed sunset at the Gateway and she even got praise for her cooking skills. Why not top it with some cosy sex? No... Let him study. Let him try his best to clear the hurdles that lay ahead of him... She laid herself down on the bed.

****

Isn't the phone ringing? Amrita looked up drowsily. Its dark. The phone was ringing in the hall. Why didn't someone pick it up? She searched for Soham.

'I am getting it.' Soham lifted himself up. Amrita lay down again.

****

She felt Soham's arms around her. He was snuggling his face into her shoulder. What time is it? Does he want it now? Not now... she is so sleepy...

'It's from Calcutta,' she heard Soham saying, 'We have to go to Calcutta Ami.'

****

The pyre had nearly burnt out. Only a few ambers glowing, sparks flickering up in the darkness now and then, being blown by a strong wind coming from the direction of the river. The wind blowing her hairs too, splashing the locks onto her face but she made no effort to brush them away. Nor did she try to wipe the tears that rolled down her cheeks in incessant streams. The body of her Baba had burnt out, could no longer be distinguished from the black mass of burnt wood that lay only a few feet ahead. The pungent smell that hit her nostrils was of her Baba's burnt flesh... She could not reach in time to see the body. By the time she and Soham reached the Ghat, Avinash had already set fire on the pyre. Two other pyres were burning; she did not know which one was of her father's. Then she saw Avinash... and rushed. He was crying, mumbling, trying to say something but she didn't understand a word. She too was trying to say something, she didn't know what, tears had choked her voice, all that was coming out of her was a wail, soaked in sobs. It was a friend of his who separated the two of them and took Avinash away. She knew why. It was not safe for him to be on the open for long. He had told Soham everything over the phone when he broke the news. That Baba's body was found beside a railway track, that he had been stabbed to death. Who did it, he could not say. Only said that Baba had been receiving death threats since one of his articles were published in Anandbazar last month. He was warned not to write the second part of the continuous series. But Baba went ahead with it. The threat came again, in form of an anonymous letter thrust into their mailbox, this time it included the entire family. But Baba had gone ahead with the third installment, it was published last Sunday. He had gone to college as usual on Monday but did not return on time. They were beginning to worry when a phone call came – anonymous – saying that his dead body was lying on the tracks near Dum Dum Station. They hurled abuses at Avinash who had received the phone and told him save his skin before they could get their hands on him and the others in the family. Avinash had fled with Aunt, the two were hiding at some undisclosed location; the police too had advised the same. The police had brought the body to the cremation ghat after post-mortem, Avinash had come out of the hiding briefly to set fire on the body - forcing her mother to stay back behind against her wishes. Now he was gone, his friend had taken him away.

They did not tell him anything. About the death threats, about the articles Baba had written. What made him so bold, to defy threats to his life? He was threatened earlier also, when she was in Calcutta, but then he stopped giving lectures at Calcutta seminars and stopped writing on newspspers. How could he gather so much courage this time? ... Was it because of her? The fact that she was no longer in Calcutta, safe with her husband in far away Mumbai? Did her absence made him bold enough to go ahead with what he thought best? She felt Soham's hand clasping tightly to her shoulder. Is he telling her it's time to leave? No, she won't leave! She won't leave now!

Why did they kill him? He did no harm to anyone. He never took sides, nor was in anybody's payroll. He was just an economist, just an economist voicing his opinion. Didn't one have the right to voice his opinion? Should one be killed just because his opinion didn't fall in line with somebody' else's? She knew her father was neither right, nor left. She knew all he wanted the best of both, had always wanted to tread the middle path. He spoke against violence, but against oppression as well. Is this the price one has to pay for remaining his own, for not showing allegiance to any particular ideology and remaining steadfast at the same time?

'Let's go Ami, it's getting late.'

Amrita looked up at Soham, then again to the burnt pyre. Her baba is gone! Absolutely gone! No more would she hear her soft baritone voice, ' Ami ma...' When she was a kid he called her 'Buri' meaning old woman. 'Don't call me Buri anymore Baba, it doesn't sound nice' she told him one day when she grew a little older. From that day onwards he never called her Buri, always Ami. And when in the presence of outsiders – Amrita.

'Would you like to go to your home? Collect something if you wish?' Soham asked once they were inside the cab. 'Avinash has given me a duplicate key.'

Should she? Amrita wondered. There's so much to collect. The books, the pens, his favorite one – the Parker, that she had presented him on his birthday. Did he leave it at home? Or carried it with him that day? No, she won't take anything. She won't go back to that house where all the fun is gone, all the people are gone. She doesn't want to go back to Mumbai either. She wants to get away from it all, from everything. Her past, her present... She wanted to block everything away, she wanted to go to a place where she could block everything away.

'Take me to America Soham.' She heard herself saying.

CHAPTER

E I G H T

Amrita noticed the pair of eyes watching her. She knew if she returned the stare the lady would avert her eyes. But how many stares would she ward off? She knew if she looked around she would find at least half a dozen eyes fixated at her, either with a slight frown of surprise above the brows, or with a bemused smile of bewilderment at the edge of the lips. She had become accustomed to such unsolicited attention by now, whether in the tube as she was now, or in the supermarket, or walking down the sidewalk. It used to irritate her in the beginning, but when she complained to Soham he had countered with his irrefutable logic.

'How did you use to look at foreigners while in India?'

True. It was even more direct, the frowns more vivid, the smiles were more giggles, if not outright laughter. No doubt a foreigner is more uncomfortable in the streets of Calcutta or Mumbai than an Indian in New York. How often had she and her friends 'oooohed' noticing blue eyed, blonde couples walking in the pavements of Chowringhee embracing each other and 'chhhheed' noticing their sleeveless, shoulderless, thighless dresses. And if a black 'African' happened to fall in the line of their gaze, her friends would fall over each other giggling aloud looking directly at the curled hairs and broad noses and thick lips without even caring to think how the man felt. She had also heard people – always men - making catcalls at 'Negroes' in Calcutta streets. From a safe distance though, they very much aware of the fact that their average five-five paunchy builts were no match to the six and above strong muscular structures of the targets of their lampoons. She had never heard people giggling at her in her few months in New York or passing comments... only once while sitting on a bench at the Central Park with Soham she saw a little girl and her brother staring at her with round eyes forgetting to kick the ball lying at their feet and as soon as they saw their mother approaching the little girl shouted 'Look Mama look! The lady is wearing a curtain!'

Both of them had laughed out. The mother smiled embarrassed, explaining her kids that it was sari that Indian women wear. Not all Americans were that well informed though. Many a times, she was stopped in the streets or in the aisle of supermarkets by women who wanted to know what she was wearing, feeling and appreciating the exotic beauty and texture of the cloth. But what made them more curious was the red powder between her hair, and she was often at pains to make them understand the story behind it. Now she had become clever enough to camouflage it skillfully, keeping it to a bare minimum, but still people did not fail to notice, especially in tubes where one is forced to look at fellow passengers sitting opposite, like the old lady sitting opposite her.

She could do nothing about the sindoor, she had to wear it all her life as long as she remained the wife of Soham Ray, but she had decided to do away with the sari. She knew Soham would have no problem if she switched over to jeans and tops, the problem lied within her for her own mental block. In Mumbai among her in laws she had steadfastly refused to wear western dresses, had worn once only, the gown at her wedding reception but now such adamancy seemed foolish. Had she remained at home most of the time it would have been different, but now she had to commute daily to attend her classes at the University, she had no option now. She would no longer delay the decision. The paper bag on her lap contained the garments she had bought from a store at Crosby Street.

Apart from her sari there was another part of her that she might have to do away with pretty soon- her own name. Amrita was losing the battle to Amy, all the students and professors at her class called her Amy, she had given up in her effort to rectify the fatal mispronunciation that threatened to change the very foundation of her identity. Her husband and a few Bengali acquaintances were the last posts remaining, but for how long she was not very sure of. She herself was fast losing the discomfort of responding to her new name despite the sadness of losing the one that her father had given her. America was encroaching upon her – slowly but surely - she could feel it in her bones.

But there were certain things she could never do however long she stayed in this country. Like what that pretty girl sitting beside that old lady doing- applying lipstick looking at a hand mirror in full glare of the public. This is impossible for her, or for any Indian women. She had seen women doing the same at her in-laws parties, Miss D'Souza her fourth grade English teacher at Lady Brabourne did the same in between taking grammar lessons. But doing it in a public transport was something no women would ever contemplate in India. One thing she had realized; Americans did not care much about what others think of them. For them individuality is a big issue. They would not restrict their instincts or their behaviors in accordance to what others say or think of them. If they want to do something they would do it. In India it is just the opposite. You dress, you eat, you buy, you walk, even the way you breathe always bothered about what others were thinking of you,except of course, when it comes to responding to the call of nature. No amount of public scrutiny would dissuade the Indian male to stand in front of a wall and let the torrent flow. No compromise with individual freedom there. She had seen Americans kissing in public, caressing each other in public – males caressing males, females caressing females - in public - without any embarrassment, rather adding to her embarrassment. And on one occasion she had seen women at a feminist rally walking with nothing covering their chest, their breasts all exposed to public visibility! It was no doubt a shocker. She averted her eyes immediately and when she saw Soham had not, she was mad at him. But they had never come across a single American male urinating in public and that was a big relief. 'It's better making love in public than urinating,' Soham observed, 'at least the environment is not polluted.'

The train was slowing down, her stop approaching. Amrita got up. Stepping out to the platform she felt a slight flurry of butterflies in her stomach. She had to climb the escalator now-all by herself. It was another new American experience for her. She had stumbled over the first time she stepped on it. Soham had grasped her from behind preventing her from falling. Next time she headed in the opposite direction, for the steps. But Soham brought her back to the escalator again. 'There's no way you can escape the escalator in America,' he warned, 'it's everywhere, you can't hide from it. Same applies to many other things. Better face them head on.' He made her climb up and down several times in few public view, first two or three times accompanying, holding her arm, and then forcing her to do it herself. She was very much embarrassed to be treated like a school girl but to her relief noticed that no one was watching, everybody is too busy going their own places. Now she was capable of ascending and descending without any hitch, but with her sari end touching her heels her heart beats a trifle faster than usual every time she took her first step. Another reason to change to jeans.

Getting back home Amrita dropped the plastic bag on the sofa. She too dropped herself on it, putting off the desire to make some tea for her. She sighed remembering the evenings that were spent in their large balcony at Calcutta drinking milkless Makaibari tea made and handed over by the cook. No such luxury here. Their two room apartment on the first floor of the three storey shingled house was not only small, it had no balcony. Never before in her life she had lived in such a small place. Her in-law's house in Mumbai was a luxurios mansion but her father's house in Gariahat was by no means small either and both had ample balconies, and terraces too. This house did not even have a terrace, the roof was thatched. Soham was almost apologetic when he brought her here from the airport one wintery evening five months ago, eight months after he himself had come here. She was shocked by the smallness, but did not show. Size did not matter, she told herself, as long as there was peace. She had found no peace in Mumbai. The companionship that had sprouted between them drinking coffee in a cloudy Calcutta afternoon found no nourishment among the spacious rooms and halls of Malabar Hill, got stagnant amidst the claustrophobic comfort and decorum and was on the verge of getting stale. They could rejuvenate it here, she told herself, even in this two room apartment, however small it may be.

They had indeed found peace in each other within this seven hundred so square feet, despite the lack of comfort that they had been unable to buy for themselves yet. But it did not come without the extra effort that she had to invest. Adjustments had to be made that were quite difficult at times - both in her daily routine and in her mindset – to transform the lazy, fish bone chewing, siesta loving girl into a hyperactive, 5 a.m. to 9 p.m woman. Things that she thought she would never have to do in her life had now become a part of her daily chore. Cooking, washing, putting up clothes on the line, picking them up again, ironing, cleaning – things she did only occasionally and purely out of choice both at her father's house and at her in-laws had to be done singlehandedly and on a daily basis now, without much help from Soham. Things had become even more difficult for her since she had joined her Radiology

Masters classes at CUNY Graduate Center. Now she had to wake up at five, come winter, come summer, prepare breakfast and tiffins for both, see off Soham and leave for her classes by eight, then returning home at six in the evening doing some shopping on the way, then prepare supper. It was not before nine, nine thirty, that she could drop to the bed, tired, exhausted, getting more exhausted meeting the demands of the body, then going to sleep. On weekends, all the cleaning and washing had to be done, Soham used to offer an helping hand in the beginning but now he had begun to bring his studies home, spending the Sunday morning and afternoons reading and taking notes from Medical journals keeping himself updated of the latest from the Medical world. He wanted to make it to the big league and she had no intention of becoming a hurdle, she was not complaining. Her only consolation was the fact that Soham too had made adjustments, never complaining if the rice got burnt at the bottom, or the meat not cooked well enough. And on Sunday evenings it was he who ironed the clothes, including her three yards cotton saris crumpled by starch. Hopefully her switching over to jeans he wouldn't have to handle the saris anymore, irritating himself in the process.

Technology had been of some help too. Though they did not have a washing machine yet – more because of lack of space than money - she need not have to wash clothes by hand, the only thing she had never volunteered to do at her father's house, always leaving it to the servants. The public washing house two blocks away was the place she went now. Putting the clothes into one of the six giant washing machines she waited patiently watching the clothes swirl in the foamy liquid through the glass door along with other women and their little kids, both white and black. It would be unthinkable in India. Daughter of renowned economist Swarnendu Sen washing clothes in public; America had brought her to the ground. If she ever had any class superiority in her, America had washed it off. Like the stains in her clothes, washed off by the great churning going on inside the huge machines.

The phone was ringing. Amrita lifted herself from the sofa and picked it up. Soham. Coming with a couple of friends of his.

'Both Americans.' He did not forget to mention. 'Want to taste homemade Bengali food. Make it less spicy.'

Amrita peeked into the refrigerator. No meat, she had to go to the store now to buy chicken, or should she buy mutton? Mutton is better, she is more comfortable cooking mutton. But making it less spicy to suit western tongues wouldn't be easy. Making meat tasty with less spice was an art that she hadn't been able to master. Aunt's advice would have helped, but she was not going to make a trunk call to Calcutta for that.

She would go to the store wearing her jeans and top. Amrita got rid of her sari and slipped into the blue denim. Then she slipped over the green T-shirt that had a blue adidas written under the right shoulder. She had picked this one, and another red one with Reebok written upon it from dozens of more flashy ones with so many things written upon them. On one she saw was written 'Fresh milk available here!' Which woman would wear such a T-Shirt she wondered. But then she remembered what she saw in that feminist rally. If they could walk topless in rallies revealing the source they could surely advertise what was available in them.

Standing before the mirror she looked at herself from different angles. Now she had become modern woman... the only thing that remained... She lifted both the sleeves to her shoulders. Now!.. She raised both her hands to the back of her head and lifted her hairs, twisting her torso a bit... Now she looked like one of those models on the cover of Vouge didn't she?... Oh! Has she gone crazy! Suddenly Amrita felt shy of her image on the mirror. Dropping her sleeves back she moved away quickly.

The counter woman was surprised to see her in jeans and T-shirt.

Smiling and nodding she expressed her approval. Amrita bought one kilo mutton, garlic and potatoes wondering whether the foreigners would like potatoes in mutton curry.

On her way back she heard sound of choir coming out from the church that lied halfway between the store and her house. It was an all Black Church, she had discovered one Sunday morning when out of pure curiosity she went through the gates to see what is going on inside. To her surprise she found all those present inside were blacks, and the one making the speech from the Dias with a microphone in one hand and the Bible on the other looked more like a boxer in a dark suit intimidating his mesmerized audience with what sounded more like a battle cry than a religious sermon. He was uttering a phrase pitching his voice up, then asking a question to the audience who were responding raising up their hands, saying 'yeah' in unison. It went on again and again. The environment was all charged up – as if they would be Haroldhing out for crusade any time. She came out quickly wondering how in the name of Christ - who looked so peaceful in photos and idols – one could whip up such war-like hysteria. She had gone inside Churches before while in Calcutta with her Christian friends, all Catholic Churches with idols of Jesus and Mary and other Saints standing all over. She had heard priests adorning white robes lecturing from the pulpit in a peaceful manner and smiling, never loud, never intimidating. She found no idols in this Church, not even the Cross, as one would find in Protestant Churches. Later Soham explained that this was an Evangelic Church with no connection with Rome or England. But what surprised her most was the absence of any white men among the audience. She was well aware of the black and white divide in America but that even their God is divided on racial lines she did not know before. No different from her country where in many Hindu temples lower caste people were not allowed entry.

She was able to finish cooking the mutton curry just in time. Soham arrived at eight with his colleagues. Amrita felt a little nervous, this was the first time any American guests would be visiting them. They had welcomed Bengali friends in these two rooms before, and non – Bengali Indian friends too but never pure Americans. She looked around the room once again before opening the door to see if everything's in order. Soham's eyes brightened up seeing her in her new avatar, he uttered a silent 'wow!'.

Rob had typical American Caucasoid features, tall, white, brown hairs – a bit lanky. Graham was somewhere between white and brown, small curly African hair. Colored – as they call here. His English pronunciation was different too but now she understood most of what Americans speak. She had problem before, Soham too. Once, a few days after her arrival at New York, they were walking along a Manhattan street, she was looking upwards simply awed by the massive sky kissing heights. Suddenly a young black guy stopped before them and beaming with his white teeth flashing said 'Fitchapila! Fitchapila!', then ran into a building. They were stupefied unable to comprehend what the guy said.

'Crazy or what!' She had said looking at Soham.

They went on looking, her gaze still upwards. A couple of minutes later they heard the same words, 'Fitchapila! Fitchapila!' They saw the same man, beaming like before brushing past them. They were totally confused. And very much irritated. What did the man mean? They argued between them. Was it a racial slur, or a sarcasm? The confusion kept lingering in their mind, Soham opened the dictionary coming back home but found no mention of the word Fitchapila. Unable to get rid of the thorn they asked Mrs. Simpson their ground floor neighbor, next day, while she was hanging her clothes on the line at the yard. She frowned and asked what was the context. They told her and she laughed out.

'The man was telling you to fetch a pillow, so that you can lie on the side walk and enjoy the view above!' The old lady cleared their confusion at last.

Both Rob and Graham turned out to be quite friendly, she had no problem in communicating with them. A bottle of Champagne that they had brought with them was opened, she took a sip too. An act that she considered almost profane in Calcutta and undesirable in Mumbai seemed no big deal in this foreign city among foreign friends.

They were all praises over the Mutton Curry but she doubted whether they really liked it. Supper over they sat on the sofa and chatted. The three young doctors talked of their profession and of their dreams. Rob talked about his desire to work with the United Nations, Soham said he wanted to run a hospital of his own someday, Graham said he would rather go to South Asia, preferably Bangladesh to help out the poor people there. That made Amrita feel a bit guilty, they had come to America leaving their sick, impoverished country behind, while someone from this country of prosperity desired to go to their impoverished land to help the poor people there. She wondered what Soham thought of that.

They left late. Soham helped her to wash the dishes.

'You know what Ami,' he said scrubbing a plate with the sponge, 'we can achieve almost anything in this country. No red tapeism here, no oiling the authority. Everything is possible here,' his voice rose, 'You can hope! You can make things happen! I will make it big here you see. I will make it really big!'

'And what shall I do?, Amrita asked.

'You? – You will do your job of course... and raise our kids.' Soham paused. Then he said with a smile. 'And help me make it big.'

CHAPTER
NINE

What's the time now? Amy looked at her watch. Half past one. Martha should have fed Oni by now. She had specifically instructed Martha to feed her by one. But had she? She was doubtful. Most possibly she was watching some raunchy soap on TV, or listening to music on her walkman. She did not like the attitude of that girl from the very beginning. Typical American 'don't care' type, always chewing gums, even while talking. But which American girl is not like that? It wouldn't have been any better if she had called someone else.

It was better at the Day Care Centre. It was not very far from their previous home at Parkchester. Oni was happy there too. She had problem adjusting for a couple of days, then she got used to it and began to like it. The principal was an Indian lady known to them and the teachers too, they taught so many things to the kids that were related to Indian culture and history. Oni had learned about Ramayan and Mahabharat and the stories of Panchatranta along with that of Cinderella and Rapunzel. She would narrate the stories she had learnt in the car on their way back home.

'Do you know what happened to Karna Ma?' She would say in her baby voice filled with excitement, 'His chariot got stuck on the ground and when he was trying to pull it up, Arjun shot him dead with his arrow!'

And if Soham returned home early and she was still awake, she would narrate the story again to his father. But that was when they were at Bronx. After they shifted to Long Island, to their third home in New York, they had to take Oni out of the Day Care, it was not possible for either of them to commute so far twice a day to drop and pick her up. They had initially planned to put her to another play school in their new neighborhood, but then Soham suggested it would be better to get her admitted to Junior School as the session began. Another couple of weeks remaining for that, they needed someone to take care of her meanwhile.

Should she call home and check on Martha? Amy looked at the X-ray plates lying on her desk. Another one left there; would take another ten minutes to write the reports.

It took less. Amy reached for the phone. It kept on ringing. Amy felt a surge of anger swelling inside her. What is the girl doing? Gone sleeping or what?

The ringing stopped. Someone picked up the phone. Sound of shuffling and dragging could be heard. Why is she taking so much time to pick up a phone? Amy felt like cursing. The girl is really a...

'Hello...'

A soft voice was heard at the other end. Amy's heart jumped and melted at the same time. Her baby! Her little Oni! Saying hello to her on the phone!

'Baby? Is it you?' Amy asked fondly.

'Ma?'

'Oh Baby! Where is your Martha Auntie?'

A silence on the other end. Then Oni spoke again in her sleepy baby voice.

'She is playing with Uncle.'

'Uncle? What uncle?'

'Uncle Tim.'

It took a couple of seconds for Amy to realize what was going on. Blood shot to her head. The girl had turned out to be wilder than she had thought.

'Will you please call your auntie baby?' Amy told her kid.

'Yes Ma.'

She heard Oni keeping down the receiver on the table. A surge of warmth flooded her heart. The little girl who only a while back could only say Ma, Baba and Potty and shoo shoo was now was now picking up the phone on her own and talking to her Ma... How time flies by!

But that girl! What is she doing? The warmth melted into rage as Amy thought of the baby sitter. What uncle Oni was talking about? Has that girl brought a boyfriend into the house? Playing with uncle! What is happening here?

'Yes Maam?' Martha's voice was heard on the receiver.

Who else is there in the house! Amy wanted to scream but did not. It wouldn't be right. These girls could get pretty bitchy at times. If she yelled at her now she could vent her wrath on her baby.

'Did you feed baby Martha?' She asked in a cold voice.

'Preparing Maam. Will be ready in a minute.' Apt came the reply.

She was lying. Amy took a breath to cool her nerves.

'I told you to feed her by one, didn't I?'

'Will do right now Maam.' The girl replied in a gum chewing voice.

Amy put down the phone. A feeling of helplessness overcame her. If only she could go to her baby now. She would call some other babysitter tomorrow. This one is totally irresponsible. How dare she called her boyfriend in? The thought made her ears burn. The guy is still there... What are they doing in front of her baby? Playing! Oh!

'Won't you be coming for lunch?' Patty appeared at the door.

Amy looked up at Patty Langford, her colleague and junior radiologist at the Elmhurst Hospital Center. She was senior to this smiling blonde girl both in age and designation but that had not become a hurdle to their friendship. Patty was now a family friend, often visiting their house with her newly wed husband Sam. She was very fond of Oindrilla, gave her a big teddy at her third birthday. Oindrilla too liked her Patt auntie a lot, always wanting a piggy back ride whenever she came to their home.

'What's the matter Amy?' Patty asked, 'You seem to be off mood.'

Amy told Patty about the baby sitter.

'I need to look for another one,' She shook her head in indignation. 'This one is too hot to handle!'

'Then better look for a granny!' Patty suggested with a chuckle, 'Any young girl as a babysitter would bring her boyfriends into the house. I did when I sat kids during my high school vacations. No big deal.'

Amy looked at Patty and sighed without showing. It is in these moments that she felt so helpless in this country. Everything is so different here; the mindset in particular. Her little girl's babysitter doing God knows what in her living room in front of her kid and it's no big deal! It would be no less than a scandal in Calcutta - a young girl bringing a guy into the house! But here it is a way of life! Even the concept of babysitters is non-existent back there. There is always someone in the house to look after the kids. And even if there's no one, the kids could be safely deposited to the neighbors who would take care of them till the parents returned, feeding the kids, bathing them, even pottying them absolutely free of cost, just for the sake of neighborly love. Here, even if she called the girl next door to look after Oni for a couple of hours she had to be paid no less than two dollars for that.

'Are you coming or not?' Patty hastened.

Amy rose from her seat reluctantly. Her appetite was gone. Her baby did not have her lunch at the right time, she did not feel like eating herself.

****

'I don't like Martha.' Complained Oindrilla, the moment her nanny was gone and she was alone with her mother.

'Why baby?' Amrita asked.

'She doesn't play with me. Always tell me to sit quiet. She scolds me!'

'Why did she scold you?'

'I dropped the ice cream on the floor. She didn't give me another one.'

'I will get you one dear. Do you want another one now?' Amrita asked.

Oindrilla shook her head in eager consent.

Clinging on to her mother she licked the cone with great satisfaction. Amrita caressed her hair with great fondness. This little thing was even more little not so long ago. On one cold February morning she came to her lap, lighting up her world. It had been a long wait, a pretty long one. Seven years to be precise. They had chosen not to have a baby for the first three years of marriage. Coming to America both got busy, first in their studies and then in their jobs delaying the desire to be three farther and farther. And when they decided to have it finally, discarding their habits with contraceptives, they found it was not coming. She had developed complications and it took innumerable visits to clinics and specialists and many more nights and days of painful longing till finally one day while frying fish in the kitchen her head spinned, and she emptied herself on the sink. Much had changed by then. They had achieved things, or rather Soham achieved things taking him closer to his dreams. He had graduated himself from a junior doctor at Brooklyn Hospital Center to a senior consultant and then set up his own clinic at Queens, earning loads of money and reputation in the process. They had moved out of the two room rented apartment at Kensington and bought a house for themselves at Castle Hill Avenue in Parkchester, East Bronx; not a mansion or a villa, but big enough to be comfortable, with a porch and a backyard and a garage that housed two cars. A Honda Civic – that Soham used and a Renault that she took to her job at Elmhurst Hospital where she now worked as a Senior Radiologist, climbing the ladder one step up from a Junior Radiologist, the designation she had when she joined the hospital after completing her M.D.

America had given them all they had desired, but the one thing that could be achieved without migrating to a country, without much effort, only by a spell of love followed by a spell of pain, had eluded them for years and without it all their achievement seemed meaningless. Getting back to bed after a hard day's work followed by routine love-making, they lied side by side sleepless in the dark surrounded by a consuming hollowness and waking up next morning they immersed them into more work to get rid of the feeling of helplessness only to make it more acute at the end of the day. Passing by happy, healthy American families full of life and children, in parks and in malls, their hearts twitched in silent pain; she would pass by houses and would look at a tricycle lying at the porch or a plastic pool on the yard and would feel the dryness within her suffocating her very existence. Nothing seemed to help.

The changing colors of the Grand Canyon seemed monochrome, the night spent under the tent at Yellowstone seemed no different from the nights spend under the shingled roof at Castle Hill Avenue. Life was fast becoming a monotonous slog.

Then she came. The prayers kept at the Kali Temple at Baldwin and the blessing of the Mother goddess of Kalighat via the dry red hibiscus made 'blessed' at her stony feet and sent by aunt via airmail seemed to have worked. The heaviness of pregnancy, the pain of labor was almost pleasurable compared to the dry days of unbearable barrenness. She came back from the hospital pressing the little ball of flesh close to her chest. Suddenly life was colorful. The waking up in the middle of the night by the shrill cry and changing soiled diapers in sleep filled eyes seemed no big deal at all. Little Oni had filled up the vacuum in their lives with her little heart-warming baby ways, evaporating the hollowness that had surrounded them before she came, cementing the disconnect that was beginning to appear. She babbled and crawled and walked and talked, in her crib, on the floor, in the bed, on her lap filling up the emptiness of the house and of their souls, bringing them closer together like never before. Days passed into months, months into years; the little ball had grown into a beautiful little girl who ran to hug her mom and dad every time they returned home from work, recited rhymes that she had learned from her teachers and showed the dance moves that she learnt too, and cried in helpless tears if the parents happened to fight, forcing them to call truce no sooner they started. And after a meal in the evening on weekdays and anytime in Sundays and Saturdays, she sat on her mother's lap and listened with eager ears the stories she would tell. Of Sindbad the sailor and his adventures, of wise Birbal and Akbar the King, of Abdallah and Marjina and the forty thieves on whom Marjina poured hot oil. And the stories of a magical land far away called Calcutta, where her mother once lived, where everything was so good, so much better – the food and the people and their gentle caring ways – her grandmother, her uncle, her aunt and her grandfather who were dead.

'Why are you crying ma?' She would ask, wondering why her Ma's eyes would moisten every time she narrated the stories.

Now she was playing sitting on the carpeted floor of her new house, her dolls and toys strewn around. Amy watched with a peaceful heart. The fruit of her love was growing before her eyes, what the future would hold for her she did not know. Life and its progress is a permutation of genes, circumstances and luck, besides the power of will and prayers. She could not speculate about her child's will power at such a tender age, but she had got the genes of a sensitive mother and a hardworking, intelligent, ambitious father. They would provide her with the best opportunities that a child could get in this country, she was even ready to sacrifice her career for that. But what luck would bring for her little girl she did not know. The tragedies that had struck her family in not so remote past made her shudder in apprehension at times, but then this is America, where despite the alienation they were safer, they were richer – in money and in spirits. It was no less than good luck that her daughter was born in this land of opportunity and hope, where one can be the person he or she wished to be, as she and Soham had. She could only hope best for her little Oniand pray.

****

Soham returned to their bed room taking a look at his sleeping daughter. This had become a habit for both of them, always checking on the little one whenever they rose for toilet. Amrita had never liked the idea of their little daughter sleeping in a separate room, she still didn't.

'How could such a little girl sleep in her own room? Let her grow up a little, then she can sleep alone.' She had argued and pleaded but Soham was firm, he wanted Oindrilla to grow up like any other American child, independent from the very beginning. But his paternal instict was no less than the maternal instinct of his wife, the slightest noise from the other room woke him up too, he had never grumbled while changing diapers when Oni was smaller and he never grumbled now to get up and pacify her when she cried in the middle of the night woken up by some terrifying dream.

'I am not going to keep that babysitter anymore.' Amy said expecting a reply from her husband said as he lied on the bed.

'You won't get a better one,' Soham answered putting off the bed lamp, 'They are more or less the same.'

'But how could she bring a guy to the house! We can't allow this!'

'Do one thing then,' Soham chuckled, 'Employ someone else to keep an eye on the babysitter.'

Amy did not react. Soham's response was in expected lines. She did not expect anything else from her 'broadminded' liberal husband who was more than eager to assimilate into the American way of life. It seemed to be her problem only. The rest of the world was fine with everything that was happening, however gross it might be. Only she had problem accepting things, 'stuck in a middle class Calcuttan mentality' to use her husband's words.

'I've been invited to lecture at the African-American Institute Ami!' Soham said excitedly, 'I am the first Asian to be invited there! They are going to give me an honorary doctorate in recognition of the AIDS awareness Program I had conducted at Harlem among Black youths. I want you to come with me.'

Amrita did not want to respond, the thought of the babysitter still occupied her mind. But she knew Soham would be hurt if she remained mum. A big achievement indeed for the high flying doctor, though not his first and neither would be the last. She should be happy in his success, or at least express it.

'Great!' She exclaimed, 'When is it?'

'Coming Sunday.'

'Coming Sunday? But ain't we suppose to attend the Bongo Sammelan at New Jersy on Sunday?'

'Oh yes!' Soham exclaimed, 'I forgot! What can be done now? I have accepted their invitation!'

'You go ahead. We will skip the Bongo Sammelan this year.' Amrita tried to sound as cool as possible.

'Won't you be coming with me at the felicitation?' Soham asked.

'I will.'

A silence descended in the darkness.

'You don't seem to be very enthusiastic about it.' Observed Soham.

'Am I not?'

'You know better.'

She was not. She had been to these facilitation programs before, ornamenting her husband's illustrious presence. It was great to see her hubby basking in glory, she basked in it too. His pride was her pride, his happiness was her happiness, she had persuaded herself to believe this age-old conviction. Some hot shot white American hanging a medal over her husband's shoulder or pinning a badge on his lapel was indeed thrilling to watch. And even more satisfying was the sight of a house full of white, blacks and browns impeccably suited in black, and charming ladies adorned in high fashion outfits, listening to his speech in mesmerized silence, then bursting into thunderous applause. It reminded her of that afternoon in

Calcutta where before a hall full of young students her father was delivering his speech on market equilibrium, equally mesmerizing the audience with his baritone voice. She was so proud of her Baba in those moments and very much upset when the speech was interrupted by some political goons. No such bad luck for Soham. All his seminars and speeches had gone silk smooth, no interruption, no criticism, only praises and facilitation, and medals and honor. But after a point of time she felt tired and bored, especially after Oni was born. She didn't feel good at all attending the functions leaving her baby behind under the care of some baby sitter. She felt uneasy in the milieu thinking of her daughter, always worrying, always wanting to go back home as early as possible. But she never complained, carefully camouflaging her true desire behind sugary smiles and tired handshakes.

She was feeling the same at her work too. In middle of looking at a plate or writing a report, she thought of Oni - her baby qualms and antics, the sudden burst of laughter that came from slightest of wonders, filling the surroundings with sunshine. She felt like leaving everything behind, the reports and the deadlines and the programs and rush back to her daughter. The more her job was getting hectic, the more pangs she was feeling. Should she quit then? Leave her job and spend quality time with her child, watch her grow up before her eyes, savoring every moment of it, sharing all the joys and pains. She knew that was what her heart wanted her to do. Should she listen to her heart? In this country everybody tries listen to their hearts and act accordingly. She knew highly skilled professionals who had quit their well paid jobs just because they believed that they were missing something very important by not being at the their children's side as they were growing up. She too felt the same. She knew Soham would not object, on the contrary he would be happy if at least one of them would be at their daughter's side all the time. It was she who would have to make a choice. Between a job that she liked, a job that was the fruit of her years of education, her father's dream and something that was even more precious: her fruit of love, her own flesh and blood. She could no longer keep herself immune to the cries of her daughter when she left for office everyday. She could no longer put a stone on her heart when Oni says 'I won't let you go Ma. I want you to stay with me.' She would quit even if that meant she had to carry the title of homemaker throughout her life.

'What are you thinking?' Amrita heard Soham say.

'I am quitting my job Soham.' Amrita replied.

CHAPTER
TEN

Fourteen years after her daughter was born and eleven years after she had quit her job to become a permanent homemaker Amy Ray came to a couple of conclusions. First, her daughter had not exactly grown up to into the girl she had wished her to grow up into. Second, in spite of the gulf that existed between them, her daughter loved her. The second conclusion - though it should have been a foregone one-was comforting to her, but not enough to compensate for the sense of failure that the first instilled on her. And this feeling of failure made Amy sad, her efforts did not seem to have paid dividends. In spite of her best efforts she had not been able to inspire into Oindrilla the respect for Indian values that she had held dear all her life. America with its different ways had got the better of her daughter, and now that she had grown up into a teenager it seemed she as a mother had lost the battle of moulding her offspring the way she had wished to. Her only comfort was the fact that her daughter had not rebelled - yet that is - and had not gone wayward, doing her studies well, always getting good grades. Many of her Indian acquaintances in this country – that included her friends and Soham's - were satisfied with just that: The kids are doing well in school, had not got into drugs or become punks, what more could be asked for. But she had wanted more from her daughter. She wanted Oindrilla to grow up imbibing all that was good of their Indian heritage, all that she had brought with her from the land of her origin; the music, the literature, the respect, the family values. Her success was only partial at best. The long hours spent on teaching her daughter the Bengali alphabets had not materialized into her taking any interests in discovering the vast treasures of Bengali literature; the books of Tagore and Bibhutibhusan that she had brought from Calcutta years ago lied unread in the shelves. Oni had learnt to read Bengali but only just, not showing any interest to learn further - a sharp contradiction if compared to her love for English literature. Oindrilla had become an avid reader, but she read only English fiction.

When she took up flute joining her high school band Amy was encouraged. It would be great she thought if Oni could play Indian ragas on this very much Indian instrument. But her euphoria was short lived. The tunes Oni played were not even remotely Indian. But nevertheless she was proud of her achievement as a flute player in her school band and sad at the same time to see the cassettes and CDs of Indian classical music that she had bought for her from music stores in Broadway lying in their covers unheard, unappreciated. So were the expensive kaamizes and lehengas bought from Indian boutiques hanging unworn in one corner of the dresser aromated with naphthalene balls; in spite of her repeated requests Oindrilla had steadfastly refused to wear them in Indian gatherings.

But what had become more painful to her was the manner in which her girl had begun to express her unwillingness to comply with her intentions nowadays. It was cold resentment. Much was unspoken, communicated with an angry frown or a loathful glare that was not only painful but unnerving too. It was not so even a year back when her daughter was still a kid to her. She screamed then, argued and cried, but relented too with some coaxing or a scold. Things changed all of a sudden, her daughter ceased to be the little kid she used to be. All of a sudden gone were the jumping around the house, the absurd questions which had no meaning yet a reply had to be given, playful fights with dad that helped him to unwind after a hard day's work. The change in their daughter brought a change in their relation too, a realization slowly crept in that it was Oindrilla's cheerful presence, her innocent juvenile ways that was acting as a filler to compensate for the slow decaying of affection between the two of them. It was no doubt difficult to accept the new reality, Soham becoming more and more irritable, losing temper at small insignificant lapses as she became more and more preoccupied with her daughter. Then came the Internet bringing with it disaster. Oindrilla began to lock her up in her room for hours at a stretch God knows doing what refusing to come out in spite of several calls until she would lose her temper and thump the door with fury. Her attire began to change too, jeans and tops had long replaced frocks and long skirts, but one evening she found her coming out of the room wearing a skirt that barely covered her bottom and a top so tight that her breasts were pushed high up. Her lips were smeared with a garish red lipstick; she couldn't recognize her own daughter.

'What is this?' She asked in disbelief. 'You will go to the party wearing this!' It was an all girls' party that one of her American friend at school had thrown, she doesn't remember the occasion anymore. 'Everybody dresses like this' was her reply. 'But you won't. Go change yourself.' She had ordered in a firm, uncompromising voice. Oni did change but she did not go to the party. Later discussing the matter with a Bengali friend of her Amy learnt that boys too secretly sneak into such all girls' affair, and all that tight skirts and tops and lipsticks are meant to attract them. She pressed the panic button, telling everything to Soham whose response was more shocking. 'Her grades are o.k. ain't they?' Soham said taking his tie off as if everything can be considered ok if the grades are all right. Her grades were always ok, on this count Oni never disappointed her. She always remained a topper in her class never neglecting her studies and that was a matter of great relief for Amy but as a mother her concern for her daughter extended far beyond getting good grades. She began to maintain a strict vigil on Oindrilla restricting her movements, no more wearing revealing clothes even when in home, no more watching FTV, no more attending parties, she even prevented her from going to malls with friends and started accompanying her to the swimming pool where boys too came. 'You're going too far,' Soham had warned her but she didn't care. She had become paranoid about her daughter, all her waking moments were spent thinking about her. Oindrilla resisted and rebelled as much as she could, often by skipping meals or by not talking to mother for days together. She even gathered courage to argue with her. 'What's wrong in being sexy?' she once asked in the presence of both her parents and a couple of close family friends in the midst of a conversation they were having about western values. All four went silent for a moment then their friends burst into laughter. Soham was smiling too but his eyes were on Amy who was not smiling at all. After they were gone Amy had a one to one conversation with her daughter. Her head was burning but she tried to be reasonable.

'What do you mean there's nothing wrong in being sexy?' She asked looking straight at Oni.

'What's wrong in it? Every girl wants to be sexy.' Oni replied without a flinch looking straight back into her mother's eyes.

'Do you?' Amy asked.

'Yes.'

'Why?'

'Because I want boys to look at me.'

Amy was at a loss of words. She didn't expect her daughter to be so straight forward.

'Didn't you ever want boys to look at you?' Now Oindrilla was asking her.

Suddenly Amy felt amused. Her little was no longer little she knew but that she would be asking her mother whether she liked boys to look at her or not was no doubt beyond her. She decided to be honest.

'Yes I did. But I never exposed my navel, or thighs or my cleavage to attract their attention. Nor did any of my friends.'

'Times have changed Ma!' Oindrilla responded, 'Nowadays everybody exposes. There's nothing wrong in it, no one thinks it's wrong except you.'

There was no doubt some truth in what she said, Amy couldn't refute altogether. This was not her India. Women here do wear revealing clothes and didn't mind at all. Neither did the onlookers. When she first landed in this country she felt terribly embarrassed to look at the open shoulders and naked navels and half of the breasts thrusting out of shirts with no bras worn inside. 'Don't they have any shame!' She had exclaimed to Soham who had laughed and said 'This is America dear. Ekhane shob chole. You'll get used to it. Maybe one day you too will be out in the streets wearing shorts and tank tops. ' Amy had responded by getting hold of one of Soham's ear's and twisting it a few times. But yes, her eyes did get used to it, she no longer feels embarrassed looking at semi naked women in streets and malls and supermarkets but she never herself wore such outfits proving Soham wrong. She had stuck to her saris and long sleeved blouses and salwaar kamizes, she wore half sleeve T-Shirts (never never without bra) and full length trousers too but never anything beyond that. She had allowed her daughter to wear sleeveless shirts and tops which she herself never did, but the sight of Oindrilla coming out of her room legs fully bare up to the buttocks and breasts jutting out of the super tight top and the red lipsticked lip like an open invitation was impossible for her to bear.

It is true 'sexy' is a word freely used here and nobody minds being sexy even feels proud to be one but she would never allow, she could never allow her own daughter to be sexy or behave like one, she could never allow her Oni to move around with half her body exposed.

She put an arm around Oindrilla and drew her close. 'We are Indians dear. We can't behave like that. I understand what you want to say but we have our own values, your mother has her own values. Won't you respect it? Won't you respect your mother's values? It will be very difficult for me to see you in such outfits Oni.' Oni had nodded under her embrace. Amy knew her daughter would not let her down. And she didn't. But if she had felt any comfort on her daughter's modest attires it proved to be the only comfort. Something was going wrong she had realised even before Oni had reached sixteen, the realization that she was losing her daughter was becoming more and more acute. She did make attempts to enter into her world trying to talk about boys and relationships and even about sex, but it all ended up in lecturing sessions and that didn't help at all building a bridge but only widened the chasm. They were two worlds, both pathetically incapable of understanding each other, she just couldn't reconcile herself to the idea of losing virginity before marriage and her daughter just couldn't accept the logic of retaining it for the big night. She soon realized that she could never become her daughter's friend. Mother fine, but not friend and that saddened her a lot, all the while she was growing up in her laps she had dreamt that one day the two would become friends sharing thoughts and ideas and secrets too but now she found her on the shut side of the door while on the other side her daughter's world grew in the cyber space of which she knew nothing. She had stopped thumping the door fearing hateful scorns and fearing losing the love that still existed the manifestation of which however had become rarer and rarer. But still when she had a severe headache Oni would care to sit by her side rubbing her forehead with her thumb and two fingers from temple to temple, but only if she had the time to come out of her room and find her mother in pain. Her grades never deteriorated though, she never got a call from her school and her teachers opinion about her were extremely encouraging and that was a great relief, she was convinced that her daughter studied too behind the closed door though no longer needing her mother's assistance. A kind of compromised truce settled in where no one in the family encroached into each other's space and it continued for some time until something happened that forced her and Soham to intrude into theirs daughter's world once again. Recalling the events makes her shudder even to this day. They were family friends, the Bhatts, living a few blocks away; Rohan was a consultant at Lehmann Brothers and Anisha worked as a librarian at St. Christopher's College, Nikita their only daughter was a close friend of Oindrilla studying at the same grade and the same school. So often the girl used to come to their house, a sweet girl with an equally sweet smile and was well behaved. Namaste auntie, namaste uncle she would say with folded palms in her thin voice and that would amuse both her and Soham, how often would you come across an Indian teenager born and brought up in America greeting elders with immaculate Indian respect, no doubt her parents were able to pass on some of their values to their daughter which unfortunately she couldn't pass on to her own child despite her best efforts. But the girl went missing all of a sudden. The FBI came and questions were asked, they grilled Oindrilla too and all of Nikita's friends. The fact that came out of the interrogations was that Nikita was having a friendship with a guy called Tony over the web and the guy had a quite an impact over the girl. That was when for the first time Amy came to know how the internet had influenced young people including her own daughter. She was never a technology freak and had not gone ga ga when internet came unlike Soham or the rest of the world for that matter. On the contrary she unwillingly resisted the temptation of this new technology, secretly lamenting the death of old fashioned art of letter writing on paper and sending it by post, that eventually came to be known as snail mail. All she could make herself learn (and she hadn't learned much more even to this day) and that too with Soham's help was how to search through Google and how to operate an email account. On Soham's insistence and not to mention with his active help she had created an email account on Hotmail, the password of which was no secret, it was Soham who operated from the account to prevent it from getting scrapped. But Nikita's sudden disappearance and FBI coming at home and asking questions was a real eye opener, for the first time she understood what her daughter did behind the close doors.

A massive manhunt was launched and a couple of week later Nikita's body was found in a forest near Nevada, naked with bruises all over. Police confirmed that she was repeatedly raped and sexually assaulted before being murdered. They arrested a forty something White American man, DNA tests proved that he was behind her rape and killing. His computer hard disk revealed that he was a bona fide pedophile and had been posing as Tony, a college student. He later confessed that he had been posting as Tony and had influenced Nikita to the extent that she left her home to meet him at Nevada thousands of miles away all by herself. The man was sent to sixty years of imprisonment on several counts including murder and rape but that was no consolation for Nikita's parents, flustered and heartbroken and they left America for good. The incident sent a shockwave among the entire Indian community of New York – New Jersey. Parents meetings were held at community centres, she and Soham attended one such meeting. It was the first time she got to know how severely the young generation had got hooked to the Internet and how vulnerable their children could be to the predators lurking in the dark corners of the cyber space; untraceable, masked with layers of false identities. She had read about such incidents in newspapers before but didn't care to take notice like all the other parents who had come in the meeting, to all of them such incidents were some typical American phenomenon in which only young white American girls could get involved. But now the same happening to someone whom they could all identify their daughters with made them very concerned. Something had to be done but what exactly could be done no one was sure of. Surely you can't stand behind your daughter's back all day and watch her every key board maneuvers, nor can you stop her from using the net. The usefulness of this technology overwhelmingly surpasses the dangers attached to it – that was the general opinion, though Amy was not very sure of it but her own opinion meant nothing she knew very well. Everybody agreed on one thing though that they needed to talk to their daughters on this and make them aware of the dangers of the Net and explain to them how to be careful in not revealing their identities to strangers. Again Amy was not very sure. Nikita's incident had proved that when a young and impressionable girl falls for a man she loses her head along with her heart and willingly becomes a puppet in his hands. So how much all this talking will help she was not at all sure and talking to her daughter was not an easy thing to do she knew well from past experiences. 'Why not install CCTV?' Someone suggested followed by roar of laughter. But then one or two voices came out in support of the idea and then they were all discussing the feasibility of it. The idea appealed Amy too so on their way back home she asked Soham about it.

'Are you crazy!' Soham looked at her as if she is some kind of madcap. 'We are going to put camera on our daughter's room! You need to visit a psychiatrist.'

The mockery in Soham's voice made her mad. 'What's wrong in that!' She shouted, 'Don't you know your daughter! Do you think you will be able to charm her with your pep talk and stop her from all that chatting stuff!'

'You can't stop them from communicating Ami. You must understand,' Soham tried to reason, 'They will chat and will make friends over the Net and you have to trust them.'

'How can you still talk about trust after all that happened to that girl!' Amy persisted. 'You just can't talk. I think the CCTV is a good option. After all we can keep a track on what she's doing under closed doors. You may think I am mad but I do think it's the only option. 'I don't think you are mad but paranoid for sure,' Soham said in a steely voice, 'but I am not and I am not going to let my daughter's privacy breached by placing camera a on her room. And that's the end of the conversation.'

Returning home they had a conversation with their daughter. 'Oni you know we are worried,' Soham said putting an arm around her, 'This incident you know have made us very upset' - 'You don't have to worry Baba,' Oni looked up at her father and then to her mother, 'I am not going to do anything that would create problem for you. There's no need to put a camera in my room.' Amy looked at her daughter with bewilderment. How could she possibly know? Do they have any kind of network by which they know every intention of their parents beforehand while the parents always grope in the dark?

'Don't worry about me at all,' now Oni was smiling looking at the stupefied faces of both her parents. 'I have not got into any relationship with anybody and if I ever do you will be the first person to know Ma. That's a promise.'

The reassurance helped indeed. Amy's worries lessened quite a bit as Oni on her own stopped shutting the door completely keeping it a bit open and that was enough for her. She never walked in without knocking and that too after Oni consented. Things were normal again, the three of them drifted inside their two storey house as usual; working, studying, eating and also talking but always in islands of their own, always careful not to clash with each other. The fun seemed to have gone, being replaced by a compromised truce and a heaviness that hung perpetually inside the heart.

But still Amy hoped that things would improve, that one day she and Oni would become friends, all the bitterness and misunderstanding that had now clouded their relationship would disappear as her daughter would grow up into a fine young woman, and they would sit together on the porch and laugh and gossip, mother and daughter together, for the world to see.

CHAPTER
ELEVEN

Oindrilla attaining the age of twenty and nearing the end journalism and photography course that she had taken up at college much against her father's wishes, Amy began to think seriously of her daughter's marriage. She kept her desire a secret though – at least in the initial stages – so as not to antagonize Oindrilla, or to invite rebuke and ridicule from both father and daughter, only confiding her wishes to a close circle of friends – all females and all Bengalis - from New York and New Jersey who over the years had to some extent been able to fulfill the void that the loss of Calcutta and India had created in her soul. Among them the most helpful as well as most influencing on her was Kalponadi, who, though not much older in terms of age was still a didi or elder sister to her by virtue of her longer stay in America. The fat lady from Jersey always with a hearty smile adorning her plump face, and always the end of her sari wrapped around her fat layered waist was more than eager to offer advices that were not merely technical but also loaded with genuine concern for those on whom they were showered upon. And for Oindrilla, who right from her baby days occupied a special place in this childless woman's heart, her concerns were even more genuine and so when Amy voiced her motherly concern to her dear Kalponadi she was quick to lay out a detailed plan of action.

'You must think of a way so that Oni could meet eligible Bengali guys. No dearth of good Bengali boys in America. Only you have to create a situation so that they might be able to catch the bait.'

And her strategy was manifold.

'You need to throw parties and invite young bachelors among others,' advised the lady, 'or you could attend parties with Oindrilla and skillfully introduce her to the right guys. Or you could regularly attend Bengali Conferences wherever it might be and also attend Gujarati or Punjabi Conferences if you don't have any Bengali fixation.'

Amy did have Bengali fixation but she was well aware of the fact that in America race did not matter to Indian parents as long as the guy or girl was an Indian and a Hindu. There wouldn't be much difference between a young America born Bengali and her or his Gujarati or Punjabi counterparts. Very few Bengali boys and girls born and brought up in America spoke the language of their parents or adhered to the Bengali way of life. Her Oindrilla spoke a little and that too because she - and only she, not her husband - had passionately held to her way of speaking her mother tongue at home. But yes, the boy must be a Hindu. No compromise on that. She would not let her Oni get married to anyone other than a Hindu boy.

'But be careful,' Kalponadi advised further, 'Oindrilla should not have any inkling that you are doing all this so that she can find a match for her. I know your daughter, she will turn the table if she becomes conscious of her mother's conspiracy. Things must happen naturally. She is bound to get attracted to a guy or two. And the beautiful girl she has become guys will be attracted to her like flies. Don't worry, a fat fish is sure to catch the bait.'

Kalponadi's direct and blunt analogies were often disquieting if not embarrassing, but that was the way with the lady, always blunt always shooting from the heart, Amy was used to it. But what she said about her daughter was very much true. Oindrilla wanted things her way, on more than one occasion she had got a taste of her adamant attitude. Soham had wanted her to sit for Medical Entrance exams, he wanted her daughter to become a doctor like him but Oindrilla shook him out of his dreams by deciding to do her major in Journalism without giving any importance to her father's plan for her. That had hurt Soham a lot, he had wished her daughter to share his chamber with him, perpetuating the progress of the 'Ray' clinic in downtown Queens that had grown in stature over the years. She had to be careful indeed. If Oni gets to know that it was all of her mother's ploy and did not like it, then not only would she put her foot down, she would throw up such a ruckus that the peace of the family will get disturbed for a long time to come.

So it all began. All of a sudden the number of invitations from Bengali families in and around New York, New Jersey increased manifold. Thanks to the manipulative efforts of Kalponadi, but it was not possible to persuade Oindrilla to attend parties thrown by others. So Amy began to throw parties at her house much to the amusement and skepticism of Soham who was made aware of the grand purpose, and astonishment of Oindrilla who initially thought her mother had gone crazy and later thought it was her effort to make her monotonous and irritable post-menopausal life a little more interesting. Again Kalpona di played her role to think up occasions and make 'juicy guys' attend the parties. Several eligible bachelors began appearing at the house, either single or with parents. Oindrilla socialized with them freely without inhibitions or suspicions, though at times rather warily, just to please her mom who suddenly seemed to have come out of her rather glum avatar and enjoying life cheerfully like never before. For Oindrilla her mother's happiness was no less important than her own, she did not complain. Neither did her father.

Several proposals came from mothers of the bright Bengali boys or through acquaintances of single guys who were still studying or had recently settled in America. Amy was pleased to notice her dear girl attracting attention from promising males but she knew too well that it was the opposite that was needed for her mission to reach its desired conclusion: Oindrilla should find someone attractive than the other way round.

She herself had found some of the boys truly charming and had wished her Oni liked them too trying hard to look for some kind of sparkle in her daughter's eyes while she discussed American politics with the some, or race relation with other. But to her dismay the sparkle remained illusive, so were any kind of signals that could cheer her up.

She had found one guy particularly charming, a doctor, a graduate from Ohio State University and presently a consultant at the Prince George's Hospital Centre in Maryland. Soham liked him too, seeing in him his own reflection and both of them discussed the guy in bed at night hoping their Oni would find something interesting in him.

Oindrilla did, speaking well of the young doctor appreciating his sense of humor and good manners but never expressed the 'extra' interest that her parents wanted from her. Same was her attitude towards other interesting guys.

Time passed, the parties begun to get duller and duller with no outcome in sight, Amy's enthusiasm waned and her irritability resurfaced. Unable to suppress it any further she did away with the pretence and asked her daughter directly if she had liked any of the guys whom she had met at the parties.

Oindrilla remained silent for a few seconds without taking her eyes off her mother then replied in a cold voice.

'I knew it from the very beginning. It was all your ploy to get me married. I thought of telling it to you that it was all a waste of time of energy but I did not want to hurt your feelings. Now that you have asked me on your own let me make it clear to you Ma, I don't like this, I don't like this at all. You should have known it by now that I will marry when I think it is appropriate for me to marry and I will marry the person who I think is appropriate for me. But thanks anyway for giving me the opportunity to meet the guys. Some of them were really interesting but they were just not right for me.'

'Then who is right for you! What better guy would you get?' Amy blurted out.

Oindrilla remained mum, a mystifying smile appeared at the corner of her lips. That made her mother even more irritable.

'Very well then! I will no longer arrange parties,' Amy announced sharply, 'I am going to cancel the one on Sunday too!'

'No don't cancel it.' Oindrilla interrupted, 'I have invited a few friends from my college. They are eager to taste Butter Chicken and Dal Makhani. Let this be the last one, the grand finale of your quest to get your daughter married.' Oindrilla smiled mischievously.

Amy was disheartened and angry but she felt amused at her daughter's animated gesture.

'Very well then!' She shrugged, 'Let it be so. Hope someone will make you interested in this last one.'

'Let's hope so.' The smile in Oni's face broadened. 'And you will be meeting some interesting people too Ma. Some of my friends' family would be coming too.'

'Whose?' Amy asked. She knew a few friends of Oindrilla, they had visited the house before.

'Elina, George and Randolf's.'

Amy knew Elina and George, they had come before.

'Who's Randolf?' She asked.

'He's in my batch. Specializing in portrait photography... I hope you will like them.'

Oindrilla's voice quivered a bit near the end. But her mother failed to notice.

More people than expected attended the party that was supposed to be the last in the series of parties thrown by Amy over the past six months. Oindrilla's American friends had come, some along with their families, and their presence brightened up the milieu. For the first time Oindrilla seemed genuinely interested in playing host, Amy understood it was the presence of her friends and their parents that had cheered her up. Though why she invited the parents remained a puzzle to her.

Randolf and his parents – Harold and Caroline - were dazzling among the crowd. They were the only Caucasoids present in the party who were wearing Indian dresses. That White Americans and Europeans looked much more impressive than South Asians in kurta pyjamas and saris Amy had realized a few years back when she visited the Hare Krishna temple at Brooklyn for the first time. It was during Holi, the Hindu festival of colors celebrating the eternal love between Radha and Krishna. Inside the temple the tall, well built, blue eyed men and women were dancing to the tune of raas music draped in traditional Indian costumes throwing color powder on each other and up in the air, it looked as if a piece of Vrindavan had descended upon Brooklyn. The sari clad women looked no less beautiful than the mythical Radha and her Gopis, the men not exactly Krishna though, Krishna had dark skin; hence his name 'Krishna' meaning black. But the dancing white men dressed in kurta and dhoti looked no less attractive than the mythical god of love.

Randolf's mother was attracting most of the attention, from the Bengali ladies in particular, not because of the gorgeous sari she was wearing but the manner in which she had worn it. Not in the normal fashion which most Bengali women wear it these days - the free end hanging on the back - but in a manner in which her aunt used to wear; the free end hanging from the front over the chest. Everybody wanted to know where she had learnt this typical style of wearing sari that grandmothers wore once upon a time.

'An old Bengali lady taught me while I was in Calcutta last year.' Caroline replied smiling.

Randolf's father Harold Spencer was an art dealer specializing in traditional Indian art. They had three branches, in LA, Denver and New York catering to a large and growing breed of Indian Art Connoisseurs among rich Americans. He made regular business trips to India and Nepal and his wife accompanies him; hence this affinity towards the Indian culture. Not only hadCaroline learnt wearing sari in traditional - though out of date – Bengali fashion, she had learnt to appreciate Bengali food too and even knew a line or two of Tagore songs. She was too willing to recite them before the Bengali audience who were more amused than impressed to hear their favorite Rabindrasangeets being mutilated by a shrill American vocal chord.

It was Randolf who impressed Amy the most. Wearing a high collar, sheen length, bright blue silk kurta intricately crisscrossed with golden zari embroidery, this blue-eyed boy looked like a Mughal prince born in some white queen's womb. Many a head were turning towards his direction. Only a matching turban was required, and an equally dazzling princess by his side.

It would be the last of the parties, so despite her sadness Amy pulled her chin up and got busy in entertaining the guests. She went around the gathering making sure everybody was feeling comfortable. Noticing a group of Indian boys gossiping between them at one corner she sighed. None of those bright lads would be her son-in-law. Amy was engulfed with self-pity. If only Oni would have been a little bit flexible! What's wrong with these guys? Well established, or promising professionals. Cultured, Hindus and Bengalis. What more she could have asked for? Waiting for the appropriate guy! What more appropriate could she find? Appropriate time! She was already twenty-two moving on to twenty-three. How long would she wait? Her journalism major is done, she had passed with flying colors and could now take up a job or pursue higher studies. But she could do that even after marriage. In this country no woman is forced to remain a homemaker unlike in India, her decision to remain a homemaker was purely her own, Soham did not force her... There's, the young doctor Kanchan Banerjee ! Such a handsome young man! And so courteous too! How many Bengali men in America these days would fold hands and say nomoshkar...? Oni thought it was a silly gesture ... it was she who was silly not realizing the worth of this good lad. He had come again today, all the way from Maryland. Not only for the sake of honoring the invitation she was sure, he had taken a liking for Oni, even Soham had realized that. But her girl... where is she now? Couldn't she spend a little more time with him? Maybe she would find something special in him this time.

Amy looked for her daughter. But could not find her. Her friends were gossiping sitting around a table but she was not there. Amy came out to the garden. Oni was not here too. Where could she have gone? Amy went inside the hall again. She was feeling tired, she wanted to lie down at her bed for a few minutes, Oni could take care of the guests. But where was she? Amy went upstairs to look at Oindrilla's room. The door was shut. She was about to knock when she heard a voice inside. A male voice... soft murmur, A feminine giggle... suppressed laughter... Oindrilla!... Amy felt her heart thumping. Its silent now. What are they doing! Amy moved away quickly.

She dropped to a chair coming down to the hall.

'Are you o.k?' Kalpona di came forward, 'You don't look good.'

Amrita said she was o.k. but she remained seated not finding the energy to get up. Kalpona di sitting beside her was saying something but Amy did not hear. All her attention was on the stair, she wanted to see who was coming down.

Oindrilla coming down... is there a twinkle in her eyes?

Blue kurta! Randolf! Coming down the stairs a few steps behind her daughter... Amy held on tightly to the chair handle worrying that she might fall.

****

Is Oni still a virgin? Amy wondered lying at her bed in the dark. Most probably... Doesn't matter though. She was too long in America to worry about her daughter's sex life. It would be a surprise if she didn't have one. She might have worried if she were in India, where remaining virgin was still an important criteria for a girl to have a peaceful married life adding to her mother's headache, but in this country it is no big deal; thank God and guys for that. This is one thing she definitely appreciated about Western perception of sex. About the rest; free sex, boyfriends, dating she had strong reservations in the beginning, but then realized it would be foolish to worry too much about it, and she gave up worrying as Oni crossed her vulnerable teen years. But she could never mould herself into one of those American mothers who encouraged her daughter to go to a date and get thrilled to hear that she was in love and even make a cake the day she loses virginity. The Indian taboos had remained within her, though significantly modified over time, but still she was fearful that they might erupt out of her revealing how backward she was. So she never wanted to know whether her daughter had a boyfriend or not, or she was in love or not. She only lectured her about Indian values carefully avoiding the difficult subjects. The only time she intervened was after that incident in which the girl Nkita got raped and killed. Oindrilla told her then that she would let her know if she ever got involved with anybody. She had taken her daughter's assurance on face value shelving her worries to the back of her mind, they resurfaced at times seeing Oni smiling on her own sitting at her desk looking at nothing, or moving quickly into her room or into the bathroom as her cell rung and coming out after a long while, smiling on her own. She wanted to ask but didn't, in fear that the monsters in her mind might come out soiling everything and she would turn into a pathetic, backdated, middle-aged mother in the eyes of both her daughter and husband. She had only kept an eye on her grades and told herself that everything was fine.

But she could not give her the luxury this time. Her daughter was no longer a mere teenager, she was a mature woman now, mature enough to make her own decisions, and that was what terrified her the most. If Randolf was a mere boyfriend of hers of whom she seeks only companionship and even sex then it was o.k. , but what if she was thinking beyond that? Why did she invite the parents? Harold or Caroline did not drop any hints, but it could be a strategy that she had chalked out: familiarize the parents with each other, invite other parents to make it look even more natural. Then drop the bombshell.

The thought was so overwhelmingly fearful that Amy wanted to shut them off as desperately as she could. She cursed the sleeping pill she had taken an hour ago for not acting quick enough.

****

'I want to say something to both of you.' Oindrilla said folding the editorial page of the New York Times, keeping it beside her coffee mug. Soham looked up above the health page that he had been absorbed into for the last ten minutes. Amy stopped filling the extra glass of milk that Soham had advised her to drink to compensate for her shortage of calcium. She felt an emptiness churning up within her stomach.

'Me and Randolf are having a relationship.'

Amy looked at Soham. He was looking at Oindrilla.

'We have decided to marry.'

Amy felt numb. This time she saw Soham looking at her.

'Dad? Ma?'

The numbness persisted. Amy felt she should say something but words did not come. She shook her head.

'What?' Oindrilla asked taking off her glasses.

'You can't marry him.'

'Why?' Oindrilla asked, sounding animated.

'How can you marry someone who is...'

'Who is what?'

'He is not....,' Amy hesitated.

'He is not what?'

'He is not a Bengali.'

'Am I supposed to marry a Bengali only?' Oindrilla lowered her voice.

'He is not Indian! Not Hindu!'

A silence followed. Then Oindrilla spoke.

'He is a human being isn't he? And I love him!'

Amy looked at Soham. He seemed to be enjoying the conversation, coolly sipping coffee from the mug. Blood shot into her head.

'Why don't you say something!' She yelled, 'Tell her! Tell her she can't marry an American!'

Startled Soham put down the mug on the table. But before she could say anything Oindrilla go up from her chair.

'I will marry no one other than Randolf!' She said sharply, 'Make no mistake about it!'

She picked up her glasses and before her parents could say anything left the room.

'Quite a surprise, isn't it!' Amy heard her husband saying.

She wanted to burst. You are the culprit! She wanted to yell. It's all because of you…!.'

CHAPTER

Amy pushed open the door and entered the room. She did not remember how many times she had entered the room in the last few weeks. It had been one month and five days since Oindrilla had left, four days after she had announced that she was having an affair with Randolf and wanted to marry him. It was a harrowing four days of marathon confrontations, fruitless efforts of persuasion and equally fruitless efforts of emotional blackmailing. Nothing worked. She could not persuade her daughter to back down from her decision to marry Randolf. And Oindrilla could not persuade her to accept an American as her son-in-law. On the third day an uneasy truce hung over 99, Preble Street, both sides declaring cease-fire, exhausted in their efforts to convince each other. Or at least that was what she thought. Only later, next day morning at about 10 P.M. did she realize it was not truce, but abandonment. Her daughter had abandoned the battlefield, leaving her defeated.

Her favorite Jacob Jenson wake up alarm clock that her father gave to her on her twenty first birthday, that always lay upon her bedside table, was no longer there. So was the set of pens on the writing desk. She dashed to the drawers, found them unlocked. Several things were missing. The cupboard was open too, the rack was half empty. Her mobile phone that she always took with her was lying on the table, she had not taken it with her – a clear signal that she did not want to be contacted. She had shrieked and rushed for the phone to inform Soham. He came rushing cancelling all his appointments.

Five days of suffocating anxiety, dozens of frantic phone calls, and in between blame games later that they got some information about Oindrilla. A friend of hers gave them Randolf's number who told them that she had left for India taking up an assignment for Georgia. She was aware that Oni was having discussions with the magazine and that a freelance assignment was on offer. But she had said it was in Brazil, about some feature on relations between ethnic communities. She was very much opposed to her going to Brazil and had told her not to take up the assignment.

They contacted the agency and they informed that Oindrilla was given a choice between the assignment in Brazil and an assignment on socio economic situation in urban India that had come up lately. She had accepted the Indian assignment and left for Calcutta, the city of her choice. In spite of their amazement and anxiety (and it increased manifold to know that the agency too had no contact number of her, she had taken no cell phone with her and had no prior hotel booking) she was happy that Oindrilla had chosen Calcutta as her subject, and was hopeful that she might visit her uncle in Gariahat. She had called Avinash immediately but to her dismay came to know that Oni had not gone there. She had still hoped that she would, but days passed, no news of her came from Calcutta. Neither from Avinash, nor through the agency. It was such a bizarrely painful situation to cope with; her daughter of all places had gone to the city that was her own and she could be of no help to her, no help at all, she did not even know where she was staying.

How many times in the past had she secretly wished that she would take Oindrilla to Calcutta, that she would show her all the places that had been the playground of her childhood and her youth, that she would show her everything that had kept her fascinated to the city even to this day. But she had made a vow to herself years ago, that she would never visit the city again. It was after Soham's refusal to let her visit her aunt who was at deathbed. That was twenty-five years ago, before Oni was born. She had not visited Calcutta since, mercilessly quelling the desire to break her vow every time it resurfaced, hiding it under the dead weight of unforgiving sentiments.

Oindrilla's departure had washed away all the vows she ever made. The thought that her girl was roaming the streets and the gullies of her city and she was in no way able to assist her had made her mad in helpless anxiety. She had decided to go to Calcutta. Soham had tried to reason, saying it would be a fruitless exercise, it would be impossible for her to find in such a large city unless she herself contacted. And there was no guarantee that Oni would confine herself to Calcutta only. Her brief included urban India, that could be anywhere. But she would not listen to Soham this time. She would go to Calcutta, come what may. She had already contacted her travel agent. She would be leaving within a week.

Amy looked around the room. The orange and green wall papers Oindrilla had pasted with her own hands with help from a couple of her friends. Priyashri and Deborah. They were her closest friends, many times they had come to the house and stayed over, studying together in the room after enjoying a hearty Bengali supper. They were close to her too, discussed so many things with her – from American culture to Indian beauty tips and even love and relationships, but none of them had ever mentioned Randolf. They knew about him, she came to know after Oindrilla left. Oni had told them not to disclose anything about the affair she was having with the American boy.

She had spoken to Randolf after Deborah gave her his number. He informed that Oindrilla had gone to India accepting the agency job. But he did not know anything more, neither had any contact number. She did not discuss anything farther. She did not want to.

He was a nice guy, she liked him the very first time she saw her. But it was impossible for her to accept an American as her son-in law. It was a possibility that she was not willing to dwell upon even for a moment. There are certain things that cannot be compromised with, and her daughter marrying an American was one such thing. She was not even willing to give a second thought on the matter, it was a closed chapter for her. She had made it absolutely clear to Soham. He had tried to say a thing or two supporting Oindrilla's decision saying how India friendly Randolf's family was, but she had rejected his logic off hand. They might have an Indian fixation. But she knew these India friendly Americans well. All their fascination with Indian culture were either superficial or for purely self-interests to expand their business purposes. No genuine respect in it. As long as business with India is booming, they will wear saris and kurtas and make sweet namastes, but as soon as the attention shifted to some other country they would discard it all and get busy in adopting the ways and culture of their new place of interest. The typical American instinct of money making is the most dominant among them, the rest is bogus. Temporary whim or pure pretence. They wore Indian culture like fashion accessories without understanding the depth of it. They would wear a sari in perfect Indian fashion - ridiculously perfect at times - but would not hesitate to show their sexy bodies through it if the situation demands. They would make namaste in most graceful manner but without understanding or respecting the values that were dear to the people of the orient. It is simply not possible for her to accept such people as her daughter's in laws.

But she knew that was not the real reason. Even if they had true respect for Indian values – which they might well had – she would not accept an American as her son-in-law. She would not accept anyone but an Indian and a Hindu. And she was not even willing to think why.

Amy opened the bed side drawer and brought out the cd player. Oni had left it behind along with the cds of Norah Jones and Beatles and some Jazz and American Blues that she listened to all the time. Oni had told her many times to listen to Norah Jones but she didn't. She had never appreciated Western Songs, never tried to. But now she listened to the songs, playing them over and over again. They were not bad after all. The lyrics had depth, the music too. She liked Norah Jones in particular and understood why Oindrilla liked them so much. Why hadn't she listened earlier, she wondered. Was it because of her unwillingness to open her mind to anything that was new? Had she got herself stuck in some cultural doldrums that had impaired her ability to accept new things? Can the same be said about her unwillingness to accept Randolf? No! No! No! That was different. Totally different. Appreciating American music was one thing and an American as son-in-law was another No parallels could be drawn between the two. Amy sat at the edge of the bed and pressed the play button.

Like a flower

Waiting to bloom

Like a light bulb

In a dark room

I'm just sitting here waiting for you

To come on home and turn me on...

Only if she had found some Indian boy to turn her on. She had introduced so many good boys to her, but none could turn her on. Not even that doctor boy. Soham would have been so pleased if Oni would have liked him. No, instead she found an American!

I've tried so hard my dear to show

That you're my every dream

Yet you're afraid each thing I do

Is just some evil scheme...

Amy sighed. That was exactly Oni thought of her efforts, of all the parties she had arranged - that they were just part of some evil scheme she had hatched. If only she had understood that all she had done was for her good, so that she could be happy.

The phone was ringing... Long distance call! Amy's heart jumped. Could it be her! She rushed to pick up the receiver.

'Hello?'

'Amidi, its me.' Avinash's voice came from the other end, 'I've some news...'

CHAPTER
FOURTEEN

'Ami auntie are you ready?' Tania asked, rushing into the room.

Amy looked at her niece. She was looking even more beautiful today in the red dress she was wearing over her jeans. No wonder the boys of the locality had their eyes fixed on her, as she had noticed in the past three days every time she went to the puja pavillion with Tania. Her mother had noticed it too and rebuked her daughter rather uncharitably for returning the stares to a particular boy of the neighborhood.

'You should never look at him! Never!' Shruti had warned her daughter. 'I will break your back if I find you smiling at him again!'

Amy had found the rebukes rather harsh. What's wrong in looking at boys at this age? If a girl doesn't look at boys at this age then when would she?

But then she thought of her own concerns about Oindrilla. She too was very much worried of her daughter when she was of this age and had followed her clandestinely in malls and swimming pools, restricting her movements and her dress preferences, always worrying about her safety in a foreign land. But now she felt that her concerns were rather unfounded, she had been unnecessarily paranoid about Oni's growing up. It wouldn't have made much difference if she had slackened her grip a bit; on the contrary they could have come closer to each other if she had done so. She had spoilt her daughter's teen days turning her into a reclusive, introvert girl who would not open up to her mother anymore. And now she was on the verge of losing her, if she had not lost her already. No calls from Oni yet, no mail, no message.

In spite of the heaviness in her heart, she had tried to enjoy the past three days as much as she could. No matter how depressed you are, how lonely you feel, the smell of Puja hanging over the Calcutta air, everything changes. The air feels fresher and the sky bluer, the mind too can no longer confine itself to its gloom. All the three days she had gone to the neighborhood puja pavilion, beautifully decorated with cloth and thermocol, and sat in chairs in front of the dias upon which stood the ten- handed Goddess Durga in her immortal action; riding her carrier lion and killing the Asur, the half human, half buffalo demon at her feet with her three thong spear, while her lion looms menacingly over the villain. The Goddess was cool though, she was not even looking at her adversary. Holding a different weapon in each of her ten hands she looked smilingly at her human devotees who stood before her with folded hands, as if it was more important for her to please and bless her human sons and daughters than killing the terrible foe at her feet. Her more heavenly sons and daughters flank her on the dias with their respective animal carriers; on the right is Saraswati with her swan, and Kartik with his peacock; and on the left is Laxmi with her owl and the elephant faced Ganesh with his mouse – all smiling at their earthly brothers and sisters. The aroma of flowers and karpoor hung in the air along with the melodies of Rabindrasangeet played over on two huge sound boxes; the constant rhythmic sound emitting of the dhak as the drummer beat the hide with his two sticks, the cacophony of children playing around, men and women gossiping and laughing, Amrita felt as if time had stopped for her, she had returned to the olden days when she used to come at this very venue with Riya, her aunt, Avinash and her Baba, only with untainted happiness and no worries at all.

But strangely, even in this nostalgic familiarity she missed America and the Durga Puja in New York or New Jersey. She was happy there too, not the heart racing happiness of her childhood and youth that would never come back, but a peaceful happiness with Soham by her side and Oni in her arms when she was a kid, and somewhere around mingling with other boys and girls of her age as she grew up. Amidst her Bengali and other Indian brethren she almost never worried about her daughter, letting her freely mix with other Indian boys and girls, never bothering to monitor her movements as she did elsewhere. She did not for once think that even in the Indian gathering there could be some molester lurking among the crowd or some loafer could take advantage of her daughter's nubility.

But not only the company of her daughter and husband, she also missed the overall charm of the American Puja, the less perfect, yet more cozy efforts of the expatriate Bengalis. Much less rituals there, but the bond was more cohesive. Thousands of miles away from their origin they huddled and co-operated more warmly like a family in the few days of the year when they could come together, trying their best to bring a piece of Bengal in their adopted land. The interactions were more from the heart, so were the cultural activities, the songs and dances and poetry recitals and dramas. Here she felt like a fish out of water, unable to participate in the gossips among women despite the fact that many of them were close to her when she was a resident of this neighborhood. She felt a definite disconnect now; the gossips seemed so mundane, all about children and their studies and about neighborhood conspiracies and complains about mother-in- laws and daughter-in-laws depending on which group had her surrounded. And on top of that the constant bombardment of questions about her husband and daughter, some of which were embarrassingly direct, like 'How much does your husband earn in a month?'

She felt tired after a while wanting to go back home, but even at home she did not feel as at home as she had expected to be. Avinash's wife Shruti had turned out to be rather ordinary, quite different from the picture she had of her in the conversations over the phone. That she hadn't read much apart from her text books was evident from her lack of interests in anything other than keeping the house clean – always instructing the servants often irritating them in the process – and watching ridiculous family dramas in TV, almost all of which revolved around mother-in-law, daughter-in-law conspiracies. Shruti gulped them with avid interest and so did her daughter when she was not busy studying, leaving the books in the library to dusts, and bookworms that were real. She abhorred the TV soaps the very first time she sat to watch one, unable to say no to Shruti's request. What struck her most was that despite the affluence that were portrayed in such glittering family dramas, despite the superficial modernity like spaghetti strip blouses that both the mother-in-laws and daughter-in-laws wore galore and the tinkering with wine glasses and women driving expensive cars and smoking, age old Indian prejudices like caste barriers and giving and taking of dowry were reinforced vigorously in these highly popular soaps. And what was more appalling was the fact that these prejudices were getting strengthened in the mind of the viewers, while one would expect modern India to do away with such frailty of hers. Shruti, despite her wishes to make her daughter a doctor and send her abroad was secretly building up a fund so that she could meet any dowry demand when Tania attained marriageable age.

There was a palpable hypocrisy in all these high decibel proclamations of modernity and development. She had experienced such hypocrisy in her in laws house in Mumbai, now it seemed the whole of India was trying to imitate it. In America, despite her difficulties there, despite the often shocking extremes, she had not seen much hypocrisy. They were what they were. But India was more a paradox; shinny, fragrant outside, plagued and paralyzed inside. The extremities that existed here were pathetically shameful, ranging from extravagant garden parties of the soaps to starvation deaths in the news. She had seen homeless people in America too, and has seen people lining up before free soup kitchens, but had never heard of anyone starving.

'Baba has brought out the car. Be quick auntie.' Tania hastened.

'I am ready.' Amy said taking a final look of her in the mirror.

She and Shruti took the back seat. Tania sat beside her father in the front, wielding the brand new Sony Camcorder that her auntie had brought for her from America. They were going to Babughat to watch the grand spectacle of immersion; The three day festival over, on the fourth night thousands of idols adorning the hundreds of Puja pavilions in the metropolis were marhed to water bodies in and around the city in eye dazzling, ear bursting processions, shinning up the otherwise morose and cheerless Calcutta night. Babughat, by the river Ganges was the most prominent among them, majority of the idols were immersed here. When she was a teenager like Tania, she too had come to the Ganges to watch the immersion of the Goddess along with her aunt and Baba.

Within minutes of hitting the road they found themselves in the middle of the processions. The daughter along with her children returning to her husband's heavenly abobe spending the three days at her father's house in earth. Trucks lit up with neors and halogens, upon which the Goddess and her children stood surrounded by merrymaking children of the neighborhoods, rolled along in snail pace being led by saxophone pumping, drum beating bands followed by dancing men followed by dancing young women followed by walking older women. Cheers hailing the mother filled the air, so did the constant announcements from loudspeakers being broken intermittently by explosions of firecrackers. The pavements on both sides of the road were thronged with people, so were the balconies and terraces of adjoining buildings all watching the grand show with great enthusiasm. Police officers and volunteers with badges on their chest were having a hell of a time trying to bring some order into the crowd. Tania was busy capturing everything into her camcorder. Amy was thrilled, all her worries took a backseat as she watched the grand spectacle no less mesmerized than any of her American friend would be at her first visit. It took nearly two hours for them to reach Babughat, a journey that in normal circumstances would have taken just half an hour. Avinash parked the car in a makeshift car park quarter mile from the bank and they walked the rest of the distance with thousands of others. All the processions culminated at the bank of the Ganga which was now a sea of humanity. Amidst the great tumult the trucks were being unloaded of their heavenly passengers who were made of earth, hence heavy enough for the men to do the unloading; the individual and smaller statues of Laxmi, Ganesh. Saraswati and Kartik did not pose much of a problem, but the huge ten-handed Durga idols with the lion and the demon all fixed together were giving the men a real tough time. They sweated profusely as they tried to bring the Goddess to the ground being cheered by other men and women of the group. Once on the ground men women and children huddled to touch the feet of the Gods. Shruti too rushed to do the same, but Amy stood back, not wanting to get herself trampled by the crowd. She was feeling a bit uncomfortable now, having long lost her energy and willingness to mingle in the crowd. Tania by her side was busy with the camcorder, not for once taking her eyes off the flip screen. Many others, among them press photographers and TV crews were busy filming, Amy noticed a few foreigners too, pointing their long zoom cameras at almost everything. No wonder they would impress their audience back home with such exotic images of the third world.

The idols were lifted again and carried to the edge of the water. The crowd moved too. Amy got hold of Tania's arm so as not to slip on the muddy ground.

'Take off your shoes auntie,' advised Tania, who already had her shoes in one hand while the other held the camcorder.

Amy heeded to her niece's advice, took off her shoes and held them in her hand. Her naked feet pressed into the muddy yellow ground leaving imprints as she moved forward. How many years since her feet touched the soil of her country again! Amy wondered. The thought sent a shiver down her spine.

A few among the men had gone down to waist high water. Other men carefully handed over the idols to them from the embankment. One by one the smaller idols were lowered into the water, the men held the idols from the base, rotated them three times and threw them into the water amidst cheers from the crowds standing on the embankment.

Finally it was the turn the Goddess. She had to be tied to a rope to be lowered to the water. More men dived into the water and with a lot of skill and strength they began to rotate the huge and heavy idol.

'Bolo durga maiki!' (Glory to Mother Durga!) One of the men shouted.

'JOI!' (Glory!)The entire crowd back shouted in unison.

'Aschhe Bochor....' (Next year...)

Abar Hobe!' (We shall do it again!) The crowd replied.

Three circles over the idol was released into the water amidst a thunderous final cheer. Immediately after, the men in the water began throwing water to the crowd above, sprinkling them with shanti jal (peace water).

'Look there!' Avinash pointed out into the river.

Farther downstream boats floated, two boats connected by a wooden platform upon which stood the idol. The platform was pulled out and the idol dropped into the water.

'Did you get it?' Amy asked Tania.

Tania nodded enthusiastically showing her aunt the recording.

She pointed her zoom towards the water on which the idols floated. The lower portions had already sunk into the water; only the torso of the fallen Goddess floated above, her eyes looking up towards the heaven, the ten hands spread out devoid of any weapons now, helplessly asking for some divine intervention that would not come; slowly but surely she would sink into the depths of the mighty river and melt, only her straw skeleton would float above and remain floating for days, long after she would fade out from the memories of her devotees. The sight of the floating corpse of the Goddess reminded Amy of a painting she had seen in an art gallery in New York a few years back. It was by some Bengali painter, she did not remember the name. Only it was a pond instead of a river, a pond covered with water hyacinth and surrounded by dark jungle growth where nobody came, a young woman floated on the surface abandoned and dead, eyes open, looking up. The painting had reminded her of immersion and now the immersion reminded her of the painting, and both reminded her of the cold, decomposed corpse of a girl who lay on the icy drawer of a hospital morgue. She was not her daughter, somebody else's, but where is her daughter now? In which city, which town, which road, which alley... Is she still walking?

They returned late. Tania wanted to show all her recordings right then but her tired mother did not let her. It was not before next evening was she able to gather everybody including the servants before the TV in the drawing room. Connecting her camcorder to the TV she began to display the footages she had captured the evening before. The processions, the idols, two little boys fighting with each on a truck, a policeman wielding his stick menacingly over a group of boys, a young guy so drunk that he was falling upon others as he danced to the tune played by the band. Amy couldn't but praise her niece's ability to pick up interesting visuals.

'Make a copy for me,' she said, 'I'll show it to my American friends. They would love it!'

The footages by the river were equally interesting. The statues of the Gods towering over the multitude, tilting this way and that way as the men struggle to bring them down, a Goddess nearly falling upon the shoulders of her devotees threatening to crush them under her weight but at the last moment checked her wrath and pulled her up, women and children competing to get a last touch of the heavenly feet, a fat woman in a red sari slipping and falling on the mud in doing so.

'Thank God, you told us to take off our shoes Tania!' Amy said.

More footages of the crowd, people moving forward towards the river en masse, the idols being circled then immersed, water being thrown at the crowd, the crowd shrieking in collective ecstasy. Photographers flashing on their shutters, camera crew, TV reporters all busy...

'STOP IT!' Amy screamed.

'What!' All eyes turned towards her.

Amy got down from the sofa and knelt before the TV. 'Play it back! Play it back!' She yelled.

Tania grasped the remote and pressed the rewind button.

'Stop!' Amy instructed.... 'No! A little ahead... A little back... Here!!'

Yes! That T-Shirt! Purple and Green, at the far end ... 'Can you zoom the frame?' She asked Tania.

Tania zoomed.

'Pan it to to right!... Stop!'

'Oni!' Amy screamed, pointing to a semi blurred female figure on the screen, 'She's my Oni!'

Everybody hovered over the TV. The female figure was the profile of a tall girl wearing jeans and a purple and green T-shirt, a khaki backpack over her shoulder, her black hair tied into a pony tail. She was holding a camera to her eyes, that obstructed a clear view of her face.'

'How can you be so sure?' Avinash asked.

'I am sure!' Amy shouted, 'She's my Oni! She's Oni! Oh dear ... She's my Oni.' She broke down.

A silence descended upon the room. Suddenly Amy got up. 'Wait!' She said and rushed out of the living room. Seconds later she came back with a photo album in her hand.

'Look!' She said pointing to a photo.

All eyes looked at it.

Oni posing with Priyashri and Deborah. Her hair knotted into a pony tail and she was wearing a purple and green T-shirt exactly the same the girl on the screen was wearing.

'Oh dear!' Shruti gasped bringing her hand to her mouth as her bulging eyes compared the two images.

CHAPTER
FIFTEEN

Strong winds from the Arabian Sea blew Amy's hair as she sat on the garden terrace of her in law's Malabar Hill house. Following a hectic week in Calcutta she had come to Mumbai. The footage of Oindrilla that Tania had caught in her camera had them propelled to action, Avinash left no stones unturned to search her niece using all his high level connections. Four days later a piece of information from the Calcutta police had them rushing to a hotel called NoorMahal in downtown Calcutta. It was in Esplanade area - the den of low budget backpacker foreign tourists - a small two storey dilapidated hotel hidden in one of the narrow lanes. The receptionist at the ground floor was a paan chewing, bearded Muslim wearing a white cap, his lips red with paan juice, eyes blackened with soorma in typical Muslim fashion. The other people standing near were of similar background, and the couple of foreign tourists sitting at the sofa looked like hippies, both the male and female wore nose and earrings and had tattoos on their arms and backs. The girl even had a belly button ring. Amy's heart that had never stopped racing since she discovered her daughter on the video footage, began to pound. Why of all places her daughter had chosen this hotel, she wondered in blood chilling fear. The receptionist did not even turn the register that lied open in front of him. The mere mention of Oindrilla Ray brought a smile on his face.

'Bangali American Madam? She left yesterday noon.'

'Do you know where?' Avinash asked.

'Mumbai.' Replied the man adding some paan masala into his mouth.

Amy asked if they could go into the room in which Oindrilla was staying.

The man frowned at her for a while.

'You are her Ammi?' He asked.

Amy nodded.

'We have cleaned the room. You won't find anything there. Still you can have a look.'

The man called a boy and handed over a key to him. 'Show Madam 212,' he instructed.

The boy took them to the upper floor. At the end of a small corridor covered was Room no. 212. A small square whitewashed room with a single bed and a table. A small TV rested on a shelf on the floor. The floor was covered with cheap pink colored carpet that was torn at one corner. Why on earth this hotel? Amy wondered again. Weren't the agency paying her? She opened the cupboard. Nothing inside.

'What are you looking for?' Avinash asked.

Amy did not reply. She did not know. Her daughter was in this room not even twenty-four hours back; she slept in this bed, walked on this floor. The very thought brought a sense of warmth within her, and a sense of loss. If only they had come a day earlier! Oni was almost within her grasp. Even now she felt so near, she could almost feel her presence. Yet she is so far, beyond her reach, beyond her touch. She looked for some sign, some smell, that could tell her that her daughter was here, in her flesh and blood. It would mean nothing but at the same time mean a lot.

Amy went into the bathroom. Noting here too. She opened the shelf above the basin. It was empty. No, something lied at one corner! Something white... Dental floss! Amy picked up the packet. Protex! The one they used at home!

'Look! This floss!' Amy showed Avinash, 'Oni uses this floss! We all use it! Oh dear she was here!'

'And she is well. You need not worry any more Ami.' Avinash put an arm around her, 'We will find out her wherabouts pretty soon.'

'I will be going to Mumbai Avinash.' Amy said.

She had come so far, there was no going back now. She had nearly found her daughter, missed her by a whisker. But she had found a sign, a small yet powerful sign; as if her daughter had left it on purpose to tell her Ma that she was around. She had not left, she was around and she would come back to her.

Now holding the floss in her fist she sat on the garden terrace of her in laws house. It took Avinash less than two hours to find that Oindrilla had left for Mumbai on a Jet Airways flight on 22nd evening. She too boarded a similar flight for Mumbai on 24th. Soham, whom she had called to give the information insisted that she should stay at Kalyani Nagar at his father's place, not in any hotel. His brother had good contacts, it would be foolish not to take their help in this hour of need. So she had come once again to the house that she had left more than two decades ago with no fond memories at all. Much to her relief she found both her mother and father-in-law absent, they had gone to Europe for vacation. Sujoy, her brother-in-law welcomed her warmly. Soham had always maintained relation with his family despite the fact that he too did not visit India again, so it did not turn out to be as cold as she had thought it would be. Ajay was an architect, quite renowned one having designed houses and bungalows of several reknowned people in Mumbai, including that of a couple of important ministers in the Maharashtra cabinet. He assured it wouldn't be a problem at all to find Oindrilla. She wouldn't have to go anywhere. He would do everything that was necessary to find her niece. Ajay's wife Diana was not as warm as her husband, though not cold either. It was a great relief that she was not at all intrusive and did not want to know much about Oindrilla. Their son Samrat was an impressive lad of twenty. Soft spoken, courteous and looked very studious. And he was a good student indeed. He finished his MBA with flying colors, and now wanted to go abroad for higher studies. He had his eyes set on Harvard or Yale. Amy promised the young man that he would get all kind of help from his uncle and aunt, .

Their daughter was a problem for them. Divya who was, seventeen years old was ravishingly beautiful and dangerously on the brink. That modern Indian girls were a step ahead of their modern American counterparts, Amrita wouldn't have known if she had not met Divya. With no parental control over her movements she was messing up with her life no less recklessly than many young American girls she had seen back in the states. Always wearing dresses that were starkingly revealing and smoking too, even at home, she had an attitude that exceeded even the most daring brats portrayed in the glossy TV soaps. And what was more disturbing was the fact that she was into drugs. Not long ago, she was caught by the police along with dozens of other high society boys and girls in a rave party in one of the many popular discotheques in Mumbai. She was also dangerously on the verge of getting physically abused when the police had raided the discotheque Ajay had her bailed out. But not even a month had passed since the incident, she was at it again; regularly going out in the evenings, applying mascara and dressed in sexy outfits; hanging around with the spoiled brats of the higher societies. It is now that her parents had begun to worry fearing that things have gone beyond their control and it was too late now to bring their daughter back on track.

Amrita was appalled to find her niece in such a state wanting to ask her parents why it came to this, was their no parental control? But she feared that she would sound too intrusive and her queries would provoke queries from the other side about her own daughter that she wouldn't be comfortable at all in answering.

But she was relieved all the same that in spite of bringing her up in a foreign land all by her own she had not let her daughter go wayward. And though she now felt that she had been excessively strict at times and embarrassingly intrusive on others, she had not let her daughter lose her way. Today if Oni was no longer with her it was not because that she had fallen into some dark abyss from where it would be impossible to find way up, but because of reasons of the heart on which she had no control. And she couldn't really be blamed for that. It was not possible to calculate and fall in love with the right person. All the guys he had invited to parties, even if Oindrilla had liked any one of them and decided to marry there would be no love in the relationship. Like most arranged marriages made in this country it would be a marriage of convenience where love would take backseat. Like her own marriage with Soham. There was no love initially, only a deep willingness, and a bond that grew gradually over the years that could not be given any definition, no need to be given any definition. Did she want her daughter to follow the same line? Or that her cousin Riya had followed? Sacrificing love for security? It wouldn't be security in her daughter's case. Her daughter was financially independent and in America a woman could survive without the security cover provided by the husband. What was it then? What was it that she wanted her daughter to sacrifice her love for?

Oindrilla had labeled her a racist several times during the marathon duels they had after she announced her affair with Randolf. You're a racist! You're a racist!' She yelled at the top of her voice not wanting to listen anything her mother said. Is she a racist? Soham too had painted her with the same brush in the arguments they had after Oni left, though he later apologized. But he made it clear in no uncertain terms that he had no problem in Oni marrying an American. He was willing to go with any choice her daughter made. That had made her mad. She had accused Soham for being a careless irresponsible father who had no concern for his daughter's wellbeing. She even accused him of hatching a conspiracy against her.

So was this solely her problem? That she was unable to accept a white American as her son in law. Is the rest of the world o.k. with it? Her daughter is. Her husband is. And she knew many of her Indian friends in America were comfortable too with the idea of Indians marrying Americans. A few even had sons and daughters who married Americans. But invariably all of them were white Americans. In her long stay in America she had come across only one Indian girl who had married a black American. Both her parents were in a perpetual state of depression. What would be her own reaction if instead of Randolf Oindrilla would come into the house with some black guy and presented him as her would be son –in- law? She would have fainted for sure. If Randolf were an electric shock, it would have been deadly if he were a black. Thank God she didn't go that far!

Is she a racist then? Well, what else. She can't accept a white American in spite of thirty years staying in that land and the thought of a black one is preposterous. What about Indians? A Bengali would be ideal, an upper caste one. A Banerjee, or a Ghosh or a Dutta ... What about a Punjabi lad? Or a Gujarati?... Amy closed her eyes and began to draw a mind map. Soham had taught her this technique long ago. Closing the eyes and asking questions and answering them, to sort out confusions that clogged the mind.

What would be the ideal husband for her Oni?

Bengali upper caste - Chatterjees, Banerjees, Ghosh, Bose, Guha , Mitra.

What about Bengali lower caste?

Will do.

Punjabis, Gujaratis, South Indians?

Caste doesn't matter. But must be Hindus.

Muslim?

IMPOSSIBLE!

Bengali Muslim?

IMPOSSIBLE!

Bengali Christian?

Will do.

Other Indian Christian?

Will do.

White American?

No.

Black American?

Impossible!

Chinese, Japanese?

Ufff...

Eskimo, Aborigine, Masai?

Am I nuts?

That is it. Amy opened her eyes. Forget about Aborigines and Masais. Even her crazy daughter won't be crazy enough to marry an Aborigine or a Masai or even an Eskimo. In her long life she had not come across or heard of a single American or European or a Chinese or an Indian who had married an Aborigine or a Masai. So she is not the only one who is a racist after all! But a Muslim is an impossibility even if an American is a No. Even a Bengali Muslim is an impossibility. Why? There can be no why. It is impossible and that is it. A black American would invite stupefied looks and mockery from her brethren in Calcutta and Mumbai, but a Muslim would invite suppressed hate laced with painful coldness. Even the liberal Soham would not accept a Muslim as his son in law and neither would Sujoy or Avinash. Eight hundred years of co-existence failed to build any bridge.

But why can't she accept Randolf? Amy closed her eyes again again.

Can he give a good life to my daughter?

Yes. An artist has to struggle but his dad is an art dealer and quite a hot shot one and he is their only son and if he is not the kind who would not take a bit of help from his parents his future prospects as an artist is not bleak, at least he can take over his father's art dealing business. Bottom line: her daughter is going to have a good life.

So what's the problem?

He is an American. A pure white American. That's the problem.

But what's wrong with that? What's wrong with that?

Will Oni be happy? All her life spending life with a white American? Won't there be problems?

No. She is accustomed to the American way of life. She is not an alien like her. She speaks, she thinks, she behaves American. She won't have problem just because it's an American house. If there are problems they will be typical ones that can arise between any couple anywhere in the world.

So what's the problem?

ME! I AM THE PROBLEM! MY MENTAL BLOCK-

Yes it's her mental block. That's the root cause!

But why? Why she has this mental block?

Do I hate Americans?

No.

Subconsciously?

No. There is no hatred whatsoever.

Do I like Americans then?

? ? ?

Generally yes. They are good people. They have many good traits that we Indians don't have. They are more straightforward and honest and hard working, less hypocrites.

Don't they have any minus points?

Yes. They are racist too. A white American does not treat a Black American as equal. But it's not really true in all cases. There are many cases of black marrying whites and whites marrying blacks.

Bias against Indians?

There is. Soham had to face some discrimination in his career in the early years. But things have improved greatly. They have begun to like Indians nowadays. Many Indians have married Americans and are living happily. Pritha married an American and is leading a good life with four kids.

Randolf's parents like Indians too. They have Indian connections. Visits India regularly. But their India romance may be hollow, superficial. Lacking substance... But at least they can differentiate between Indians and red Indians unlike many Americans who still cant.

So what's the problem?

Suddenly Amy wanted to cry out.

They are not my own people! She screamed inside her mind. They are not my own people! I can never think of him as my own son. I can never be at ease with him. I can never open my heart to him! I cannot complain to him about anything, I can never cry putting my head on his shoulders, he can't give me any consolation... I can never feed him Fish Curry... I can never take care of him the way a Bengali mother-in-law does...

Burying her head into her hands Amy broke into tears.

CHAPTER
SIXTEEN

Oindrilla looked at her watch. Quarter past two. She had another one hour in her hand. At around three-thirty Sadiq would come in his auto-rickshaw. This would be her third day trip around Mumbai in this typical Indian vehicle that was a combination of scooter and rickshaw with a fabric roof and the two sides open. She had preferred the auto rickshaw - normally called auto - to a car taxi because of the wider view of the surroundings that was available from inside this three wheeled vehicle. She liked the jerking too, a slow continuous jerking that were produced by the friction of the wheels with the asphalt that is transmitted into the body producing an enjoyable sync, you just want to go on and on The friction at times made the lens shake a bit, but she had experienced hands; she had taken many good shots while on the move.

Sitting before the table by the window of her hotel Oindrilla switched on her Macintosh laptop. Below her flowed the busy traffic of Karve Road, one of the important roads in Mumbai connecting all the places lying along the one side of the Mutha River. In the last two days she had crisscrossed this road and other roads - and streets and alleys - on Sadiq's auto, sometimes on crowded buses and many a times by foot taking innumerable shots on her Nikon D700 camera and planning to move to Kalyaninagar today and then to Bijapur. This huge area is a true melting pot in every sense of the word, a photographer's delight. There's a non-stop movement all around, chaotic, colorful, tense; rich and superrich in their latest model cars discussing business deals or turning the pages of Economic Times, the great Indian middle class fretting and cursing, gossiping and laughing inside jam packed buses and local trains, the poor and super poor drudging along the roads and pavements pulling carts laden with commodities, or begging with their bowls. The ambience is all charged up from morning till late at night; buses blaring air horns, street vendors shouting at the top of their voice as they sold their commodities, cars, taxis, autos and buses honking mad, vying for every inch of the road. The sound of azans blurting out of loudspeakers on top of mosque minarets mingled with chant of prayers from Hindu temples; the two communities working, residing, moving side by side, not always peacefully and increasingly apprehensive of each other. Ten years ago this part of the city was up in flames, in the very street below her the Hindus and Muslims were baying for each others blood, burning shops and Mosques and temples and stabbing each other. Police too were out in large numbers, they were more busy shooting and killing than stopping the violence. It was soon after the demolition of the Babri Masjid in Ajodhya by right wing Hindu groups, an incident that had ripped apart the secular fabric of India forever. Sadiq, the Muslim auto driver narrated to her the incidents of those fearful days in vivid details as she traveled the roads sitting in the backseat of his vehicle taking photos. He was a victim too, his brother was shot dead when the police barged inside Suleiman Bakery and opened fire. Nine people were killed in the incident. Around thousand people were killed in riots, three hundred Hindus, seven hundred Muslims, a vast majority of them killed in police firing. The trust between the two communities that lived and thrived together for ages took a serious dent, more so after the serial blasts a couple of months later that occurred simultaneously in eleven places including the Mumbai Stock Exchange. More than two hundred people were killed, and many more arrested in the crackdowns that followed. The trial was still going on with no verdict in sight as the masterminds had escaped to neighboring countries and were carrying out their agendas from there.

'We have lost all faith on police,' Sadiq lamented, 'You just can't say when they would pick us up and throw us into jail leveling false cases. We are either terrorists in their eyes, or Pakistanis.'

Why Pakistanis, Oindrilla had wanted to ask. Was it because of the perceived 'Pak hand' behind every blast? Or was it because of the deep mistrust between the two communities since the days of partition when India was divided into two as the British left, the new nation born was Pakistan – a home for the Muslims – amidst bloodshed of a scale that the modern world had not witnessed before or since. Millions of Hindus, Muslims and Sikhs exchanged their countries leaving behind their lands and homes, relatives and neighbors, and stepped into an uncertain future carrying pieces of their broken hearts. But those who stayed behind? The Muslims of India? Had they all become Pakistanis in the eyes of Hindus? Oindrilla wanted to ask Sadiq, but did not, afraid of the response she might get.

But in this vast country the divide was not only between Hindus and Muslims, divisions were everywhere, on every possible lines: Religion, class, caste, creed, race, gender, haves and have not's. And the fault lines were deep, unbridgeable, causing agony and pain and anger and confrontations often violent and deadly.

But despite all the chasms, all the dissonance there is a harmony; there is a sync that had held this nation together. She had not yet understood what it is but had felt it, felt it inside her as she traveled on the roads and streets and gullies of Calcutta, Varanasi and Mumbai, and had tried to capture the essence of it in the thousands of clicks she had made in the past six weeks.

The images were all stored in her laptop, but only a couple of hundred of them she would send to the magazine on whose behalf she had taken up this assignment. And out of the hundreds she had shortlisted a few dozen that were her favorites, she would add text to these as a part of her brief, digging into the notes and observations she had taken on her notebook and on her mind.

Oindrilla scrolled through the images. This one according to her is one of the best she had taken. It was taken on a sunny Calcutta afternoon from inside a restaurant in Park Street area. She had gone into this McDonald type eatery to fill in some quick snacks when she noticed the scene. She found it so captivating that she ignored the 'Photography Strictly Prohibited' signs that were pasted on the walls and brought out her camera. Beside the huge glass window that overlooked the busy street outside, a family of four were having lunch sitting around a table. Dad, mom and their two little kids, son and daughter, having a sumptuous Indian meal of chicken curry, paneer kofta, steaming dehradun rice, dal makani, papad and curd that were laid before them on fragile china as a waiter watched over in studious obedience. And beyond the glass divide, on the dusty pavement on the opposite side of the road sat another family of four – dad, mom, and two daughters. They were having their lunch too - of rice and dal - all from a single aluminium bowl as pedestrians pass over them blowing dusts as salt and pepper on their not so spicy meal. Without caring for any retribution she pressed her shutters several times till she got the best shot. The mother at the table got upset as the daughter began throwing tantrums over something in the food she did not like and the father got involved too calling the waiter and began talking to him in animated high decibels, while on far end of the frame the family on the pavement were all eating and laughing over something. She captured the moment pressing the shutter as many times as she could before someone from the staff told her to put down the camera immediately. She did, apologizing, but by then she had got what she wanted: a piece of eternal India in all its nakedness, captured in her Nikon D700.

Oindrilla scrolled down. This one she had taken at the Monikornika Ghat at Varanasi. It is a crematory ghat by the flowing Ganges, where Hindu corpses were burnt on pyres. It was dusk, the sky turned red, the red ball lowering itself into the horizon. Two pyres burning side by side, flames blown by the winds. A boy of twelve standing before the pyres and beside him his little sister, both looking at the flames. No tears in their eyes, only a blank look as if they had not yet understood the significance of the event that had changed their life forever. A few adults stood behind the two, but she had purposely kept their faces out of the frame, focusing only on the siblings as seen through the burning flames.

Oindrilla scrolled farther down. This shot she had taken from a railway platform when she was returning to Calcutta from Varanasi where she stayed for a fortnight. The Poorva Express had stopped at this station the name of which she had forgotten to notice. It was dawn, the first light was breaking on the horizon. She had alighted from the train to take a view of the station. The platform was near empty, a few people were sleeping on the benches. A couple of chaiwallas were selling tea on earthen cups to the passengers on the train through the windows. A woman had bought a cup and was blowing into it to cool the steaming tea, her eyes still filled with sleep. She had taken a shot of the woman with the platform and the long trail of compartments in the perspective, as well as the red dawn sky. It had come out rather well. Oindrilla kept looking at the photo admiring its details. Suddenly she felt a pang inside her heart as the woman in the photo reminded her of someone. She wanted to shut the thought off her mind immediately, but couldn't. This was happening to her more and more. The more she tried not to think, the more it haunted her. It was not so when she arrived in this country. The resentment and anger within her was so intense then that she had simply cut off a fuse inside her mind that did not allow her to think of the person who was responsible for creating the fury within her. But as time passed, as she got involved with her work in this new land, breathing in its air, walking on its soil, talking to its people, the fire within her had gradually subsided. Not that it had doused fully. It was still there, it still burnt, she had not been able to forgive yet, nor forget... but she had understood. Or maybe she didn't. There were still many questions unanswered, but at least the inexplicability was no longer as painful and resentful as it was before. Is she trying to understand her mother? The woman who refused to accept the one man her daughter had ever loved. Maybe the woman looking at her from the photo had the answer. Or the little boy and the girl standing before the burning pyre, or the woman scolding her fussing daughter in the restaurant? Or all the characters in all the photos that she had taken in the last few weeks? The more she had seen of India in her viewfinder, the more the country revealed herself to her with all her complexities, prejudices, taboos, hurdles and struggles; the more she discovered the woman who brought her to the world. She hadn't found the answer yet, but had felt there was one, and this realization had tamed the burning anger within her to a placid resentment that now hovered on the edge of forgiveness though she knew that she would never be able to forgive.

She had discovered herself too in the process. If she suffered from any crisis of identity, it was gone now. That she was an American by heart and not an Indian, these few weeks in India had confirmed the belief in her. True, she might have tried to look at this country from a perspective that was different from an average foreigner, being more sympathetic to its plights, more sensitive to its complexities - being born to and brought up by Indian parents must have played a role in her subconscious. But still she was outsider. Just like any other American visiting India for the first time she too had winced smelling sweat inside crowded buses, shrugged in horror seeing people shitting beside railway tracks, calmed her apprehensive nerves before gulping the tea in earthen cups above which flies hovered, and at times just wished to run away from it all.

And this realization had made her realize that her mother too is an outsider in the country that she had migrated thirty years ago. Just like her, her mother too had viewed her adopted country from the other side of the lens, as a spectator, never being able to become a part of the story that was America. Her story had always remained India despite the comforts she enjoyed in her new land, despite the fact that she had never again visited the land of her birth. The first twenty-two years of her life spend in suburban Calcutta had casted her in a firm mould that her adopted land could not make any dent into. America might have changed her name from Amrita to Amy but the person inside had remained as Indian when she came to this country thirty years back.

But why did she try to cast her daughter in her own mould? The question had haunted her right from her early teen days as she began to resent her mother's obsession with her, and all her efforts to bring her up in a manner that was pathetically different from the rest. She had suffered because of her mother's protective instincts. She had never been able to enjoy her teen years carefree, like her American friends did. Her mother's shadow was always upon her, even when she was not intrusive and not asking questions. She was not afraid of her mother, but was afraid to hurt her, and so she denied herself the pleasures that any young girl in America took for granted. She was never out on a date and never had any boyfriend till Randolf came to her life. Not that boys found her unattractive. She had received admiring glances from the opposite sex right from the days she attained puberty, and many a boys had send her proposals either directly or through her girlfriends. But every time she refused though her heart raced, and she had sleepless nights fantasizing the dates that she was too paralyzed to make real. She had crushes too and severe ones, but again the fear of her mother's retribution combined with the fear of hurting her feelings had prevented her from taking any bold steps. Twenty-two years of her life she had wasted under the burden till Randolf came to her like a whirlwind, and swept her away breaking all the fences she had built around her heart and smashing all the blocks that had kept her mind under her mother's custody. She rebelled for the first time in her life. And when her Ma refused to accept Randolf point blank, all her resentments that she had held back all her life boiled over like a volcano, erupting after remaining dormant for so long. She had called her mother a racist, a tyrant and what not... After four days of direct face off she could not take it anymore. She wanted to run away leaving everything behind, the emotional exchanges, the slander, the charges and counter charges; her past, her memories, even her Randolf.

She did run away, but only to a place where she felt her Ma more than ever before. She had thought of going to Brazil initially but when the editor gave her the choice she knew she would not be able to say no to this new offer. She arrived in India with a heavy heart that was smoldering in fury and pain. But as time passed and she clicked her way through crowded Calcutta roads and narrow Benaras alleys, the country of her parents opened herself in her viewfinder in all its vibrant colors and dark glooms; the heaviness inside her heart subsided, the pangs of fury became less and less acute, and now she felt an emptiness within her. An emptiness that she knew was created not only because of Randolf's absence but also because of her mother's. And she had realized that this emptiness would become a part of her if she ran away to Randolf, and that was why she found herself unable to do so. She did not want to lose her mother for the sake of the man she loved.

A message beeping on her cell. Sadiq. Waiting for her in the lobby. Oindrilla shut down her laptop and hung the camera bag on her shoulder. Today Sadiq would take her to his home in the outskirts of Mumbai. It was a long distance from here but she had agreed to go. It would be interesting to meet a Muslim family in Mumbai and know about them, she might be able to capture some intimate moments too. Oindrilla came out of her room and locked the door.!!

******

'When they brought him to the hospital he was still breathing. The doctors were afraid, they were not willing to admit without police permission. I fell to their feet and begged. When they finally took him to the operation table he was already dead.'

The old lady wiped her eyes with the end of her hijab. Oindrilla felt an urge to take up her camera. But she restrained herself. It would be totally shameless, to take advantage of one's grief for a good photo. She had never clicked a person crying letting him or her know. If she had done so, she did it clandestinely, always from a distance, using the zoom lens. But if it were a smile, she usually had the person look directly at the viewfinder. Just like a few minutes ago when the entire family – Sadiq, his mother and two sisters – were all looking at her camera and smiling bright.

She had taken many other shots too. Of the two rooms in which the family lived, their modest belongings, of the verandah that they shared with their neighbors on the upper floor of this old building, the gully below on which boys were playing cricket. She also took snaps of the sisters working in the kitchen, the mother at the sewing machine, all eating kebab which she too had tasted and found heavenly. Now she sat on the bed with the family looking at old family albums. It was her younger son's childhood photo and his painful memory that brought tears to the old woman's eyes.

'He had nothing to do with anything that happened. He never hurt a soul, he was so humble. He just worked in the bakery.' Sadiq's mother sighed.

'They haven't yet been able to give a proper explanation why they went inside the bakery and killed so many people. They said there were terrorists hiding, but all those killed were innocents. They could not capture a single terrorist.' Aslama, one of the sisters said.

'Isn't anyone held accountable?' Oindrilla asked in her broken Hindi.

'Accountable?' Heena, the other sister said in an animated voice. 'In this country the police is accountable to no one. A commission was set up and it implicated some top officers. But the government had not tabled the report to this day. No government, whether Congress or BJP. Even the courts are silent on it.'

'But so many arrests were made after the blasts,' Sadiq said, 'Hundreds of Muslims are rotting in the jail. The trial is dragging on and on with no end in sight. You tell me how many of them were responsible? Maybe only a few. And the masterminds had all escaped! Why should so many innocent people suffer because of something they had not done?'

Oindrilla had no answer. The same allegation was leveled against the administration in her country too. 9/11 had changed everything. Muslims in America were a nervous lot today, apprehensive, fearful - of the Patriot Act, of Guantanamo, and of their future in a land that was becoming more and more hostile.

'We are not treated as equal here,' Sadiq continued, 'Many more Muslims were killed in the riots. But how many Hindus were put in jail? There is one leader, an MLA who led the mob that set fire to Muslim homes and mosques. He is now a minister in the cabinet! You tell me isn't this injustice?'

Oindrilla looked at the young man with whom she had been traveling for the last three days. There was fire in his eyes. Of an impotent rage that burnt inside his heart, and in the hearts of millions of his brethren. But not all rages were impotent she knew. There were rages that do not remained confined to the heart only, some rages find vent in ways that were lethal, and in turn give birth to more rages. And the cycle continues.

'This is me.' Sadiq's mother pointed out to a black and white photograph that had turned yellow with age. 'And this is my sister Jahanara. I was only thirteen then.'

'Where was it? Mumbai?' Oindrilla asked.

'Oh no!' The old woman laughed. 'This was Peshawar.'

'Pakistan?'

'Well, it was undivided India then,' Sadiq's mother smiled, 'spent sixteen years of my life there. Came to Mumbai marrying Sadiq's father in nineteen forty four.'

'That means three years before partition. Did you go back to Peshawar again?'

The old woman sighed and shook her head.

'No.'

'Why?'

'He didn't let me. It became a separate country. There were visa problems. And many other problems.'

'Didn't you miss Peshawar?'

The old woman smiled.

'I still do. I miss it every moment of my life.'

'Ammi doesn't belong here,' Amina said putting an arm on her mother's back, 'she never did. Her body is here in Mumbai. But she had left her rooh back in Peshawar.'

Like her mother, Oindrilla thought. They were no different, this old lady and her Ma. Both had left their land of birth at a young age and settled in a new land that they could never call their own. Sadiq's Ammi had left her soul back in Peshawar and her Ma never stepped beyond the little India she had let herself confined to in all her three decades stay in America... and she did not want her daughter to step out either. But her Ma did not realize that there was no question of her stepping out, the India that she tried so hard to build in her daughter was never really built. Her efforts had all gone waste.

It was late evening when she finally took leave from the family. Sadiq wanted to drop her off at the hotel but Oindrilla did not agree. It was already six, going all the way to to the hotel and coming back would take no less than five hours, even more if caught in traffic jam. Not before midnight Sadiq would be able to get back home. Better if she took an alternative vehicle from Mumbai Station to Karve Road. That would take lesser time and save Sadiq's pain of dropping her at the hotel and returning home that late.

Sadiq offered to take her to the station. It took five minutes. Sadiq parked his vehicle on auto stand a few paces to the left of the main entrance. They walked up the stairs pushing their way through the crowd to the other side of the station and stood behind a long serpentine queue. Thanks to her ladies status, it took much less time for her to get a cab to Karve Road.

'You go back now,' She told Sadiq as they reached the collapsible iron gate guarded by ticket inspectors in back uniforms. 'We shall be meeting at ten tomorrow then?'

'Sure Madam,' Sadiq smiled, 'I'll be at your hotel at ten dot. Goodbye Madam.' Sadiq put forward his hand.

'Goodbye.' Oindrilla shook his hand.

She turned back and stepped outside the gate. The nearest gate towards the overbridge is to her right. Oindrilla headed towards the gate. The moment she put her foot on the step to descend, a deafening sound burst through her ears. She felt a pressure and stumbled upon the steps. People stumbled upon her and on her sides.

She did not know how long it took her to get up on her feet. When she finally did she saw people yelling and scurrying around in all directions. Oindrilla headed back towards the gate. Through the iron grills she saw bodies lying on the floor on the other side, one man had part of his head blown off, a lady was struggling in a pool of blood, her left leg below her knee lying a feet apart... many more bodies, some lying, some sitting and moaning, parts of their skin burnt black and smoking, white flesh mixed with red... A tattered brown shirt, black trouser, a body lying head down... Oindrilla's heart stopped. She ran...

His face on a pool of blood Sadiq was lying still on the concrete floor. Oindrilla's legs felt weak. She dropped on her knees, then squatted on the floor. She struggled to find her cellphone in her handbag.

She wanted to leave! She just wanted to get out of here!

Oindrilla searched her cell... Ma... Where's her Ma's number? Didn't she store it?...1-212-706-8692...1-212-706-8962?... 1-212-706-8296.... What's her Ma's number!

CHAPTER
SEVENTEEN

Getting into his father's office - the store room attached to which he had converted into his studio - Randolf walked up to the coffee machine and made a cappuccino for himself. Carrying the hot cup he came near the window and pulled up the blind. The morning LA traffic had started rolling on the street below. Randolf looked at his watch. Quarter to nine. His crew would be here in another fifteen minutes. And Julia Simpson should be coming by nine fifteen. This would be the second time the Hollywood actress would come to this makeshift studio of his. Originally it was planned that he would shoot her at her apartment in Encino, but then he thought he would be more comfortable here and asked Julia to come and have a look. She came, and liked it immediately. He was lucky, that his father had a branch of his art shop in LA with an office and a store on the upper floor that he permitted his son to use. Or else he would have had to hire a studio paying exorbitant rent, or shoot at Julia's apartment with her boyfriend watching every move of his. He wouldn't like that at all. Julia Harlot's boyfriend was a megalomaniac in every sense of the word. That Kevin Smith was stinkingly rich and a liquor tycoon he knew, but that he was such a jerk he had no idea. How a sweet girl like Julia liked a man like Kevin was beyond him. It must be his money. He boozed almost throughout the day, and was quite infamous for being a womanizer and his rotten remarks and behaviours in bars. Abusing people, picking up fights, patting arses of bartender girls, even going to the extent of having sex with strip teasers in the clubs was what his name meant in the higher circles. And he was of also very proud of his status. In spite of her appearance in a few movies and soaps, Julia had not got a real break yet, and still not confident enough to survive in Hollywood on her own. She needed a support and a ladder to make her way up the slippery pyramid of Hollywood, and a guy like Kevin could give her just that. That she would kick his fat butt the moment she reached her goal and would have no regret at all, Randolf had no doubt about it.

Not only did Kevin disapprove of him the first time they met at Julia's apartment, he disapproved his work too.

'I don't think much of 'em,' he had shrugged and dropped the magazine on the table from a height after taking a brief look at the portraits he had done for Cosmopolitan. 'It hasn't much ammo in it.' It was terribly humiliating, but his professionalism had got the better of him, it was Julia who gave her the offer. Not her boyfriend.

'Not everybody is born with the gift of appreciating the sublime.' He had replied, looking directly into Kevin's eyes. He knew he had sounded snobbish, but the situation demanded it.

Kevin had suddenly gone stiff, his eyes flared up for a second.

'I think they are excellent.' Julia had intervened. 'You are the right person for me.' She had said smiling at him, then turned at Kevin but the smile had disappeared. He immediately knew there was a tension between the two of them.

Kevin had cooled down.

'How have you visualized her?' 'Something awesome?' He asked, smiling cold.

'I haven't decided yet.' He had replied. It was a lie, he already had a plan, but he was not going to discuss it with that jerk.

'I have a suggestion. You must shoot her in the nude. Partly at least. She would look ravishing in nude.' Kevin said drawing Julia close to her.

Randolf noticed Julia stiffen under the embrace. He didn't feel comfortable either.

'I have not decided yet.' He said again.

'Take my advice young man,' Kevin smiled again, 'It would be a hit if you do her in nude. It would be a buster shooting her topless and from the rear. That would help her a lot. And you too. And to be honest, me too! I have twenty percent stake in the magazine, you know.'

Was it a threat? He had wondered. But again Julia Harlot was his boss, not Kevin Smith. And Julia gave him full freedom. She called at night to confirm it again.

'I have full faith on you Randolf. You do it as you think best.' She had reassured her.

Sipping his coffee Randolf glanced upon the morning newspaper. His eyes got stuck on a news near the bottom of the front page. Fifty-six dead, killed in a blast on Mumbai railway station. Randolf felt a chill pass down his spine. It took him less than a minute to read the article. Where was Oindrilla now? He wondered. Could there be any possibility that she was in Mumbai? The silly girl! She didn't make a single call since she left New York more than a month back. What was her problem? She had a fight with her mom, left home, went to India. Fine. No problem with that. But why didn't she call? Not even once! And there was no way he could call her. The girl had not taken her phone to India, or just threw away the card. Every time he called he got the same answer: this number cannot be contacted. He felt so irritated at times, and so helpless. He had tried not to think of her anymore, just put an end to all this once for all. But the more he tried to forget, the more he worried about her. The love that he felt for this girl about a year back had not worn off a bit, only grown more intense with her absence. But what was the story on the other side? Did Oindrilla's feelings for him get blunted because of some reasons? Her mother was weighing heavily on her, but that was no reason why she should lose her feelings for him? Or did she find someone else in India, some Bengali guy who understood her better than he ever did? Not that there was no such possibility. Oindrilla had ridiculed her mother's attempt to get her engaged to America bred Bengalis and other Indian guys, she was not at all influenced by their Indo-American charms. But that was when he was by her side, meeting every day at his rented apartment at Lexington Avenue. He had taken her to his parent's house too, and they had spent quite a few intimate afternoons in his attic room. But never had Andy and he shared nude video chats like Marta or Richard or any of the other American as well as some of the Indian boys and girls did through the online nude chat rooms be it Chaterbate or Bongacams. He has heard of both men and women who are physically residing at a distant place, or not being emotionally strong enough to counter the societal culture and fulfill their carnal needs, masturbate using these online chat rooms. This gave them some relief towards fulfilling the needs of their bodies. They have of course enjoyed the verbal sexual chats that they had at night, but she had never spent a night with him though, always returning home like an obedient girl, fearful of her mother's wrath. But now she was all alone in a new country, emotionally fragile and vulnerable. What if some cute native Indian sneaked into her heart? Definitely a possibility, Randolf sighed. But nothing he could do about it.

The news of the blast had him more worried. What if something bad happened? Not this blast but something else, somewhere else. A young woman traveling single in India was not like traveling single in America and Europe. The risks involved were far too great. Could that be the reason behind her silence? Deborah had told him that her mother had gone to India to find her. No news from that front too.

The door opened. Julia Harlot stepped in.

'Hi.' A charming smile brightened up the room.

Randolf rose from his chair and helped Julia with her coat.

'You arrived early.'

'I always do,' the actress smiled, 'Do you mind?'

'Oh no!'

'Where's your crew?' Julia asked.

'Will come any moment.'

'Have you decided what to do with me?'

'Have some coffee first.' Randolf poured a cup and gave it to Julia. The two sat on the table by the window.

'What about some oriental look?' Randolf asked.

'You mean...?'

'Indian.'

'Can you elaborate?'

'I am thinking of using ethnic Indian accessories. Let me show you.'

Randolf brought a suitcase upon the table and opened it.

'Wow aren't they beautiful!' Julia exclaimed picking up a beaded choker. 'And what's this?' She picked up a garland made of a number marble sized round balls, dark brown in color with a rough surface.

'This is Rudraksha. Haven't you seen pictures of Indian yogis in them?'

'Oh yes I did! You want to try those on me?'

'I am going to try a whole lot of things on you, don't worry.' Randolf smiled.

'This too!' Julia picked up a red chiffon sari from the suitcase.

'Well if you are willing to try!' Randolf replied.

'I am open to new ideas. But what about the outfits I have brought with me? Shan't we try those too?'

'We shall try everything. Bottom-line is we have to bring the best out of you. Every possibility will be explored. Nothing would be left to chance. We shall make it together.'

'That's the spirit I was looking for! Julia beamed.

****

It was eight in the evening when finally Randolf told his crew to pack up. They left, but Julia stayed back. The outcome of the ten hour gruel had been highly satisfactory. Randolf had got what he was looking for and Julia was satisfied with it too. And both were now confident of satisfying the editor and the creative director of Citygirl, the magazine on whose centrespread Julia would appear. The actress was visibly happy despite the fatigue that was now etched on her face.

'Don't you think we should enjoy a drink together?' She asked.

'Do you want to go out? Or shall we have it here. I have some fine Chateau Mouton with me.' Randolf said.

'Let's have it here.' Julia said.

Randolf brought out a bottle from the cabinet and filled Julia's glass and his. The two sat around a table on the office outside the studio hall.

'It has come out rather well, isn't it?' Julia asked.

'I got what I wanted.' Randolf replied.

'You liked working with me?' Julia asked looking straight at Randolf.

'You are very co-operative.' Randolf smiled, 'I was a bit apprehensive at first you know. I had this idea that Hollywood stars are all super bitches and spare no opportunity to stroke their egos. But you turned out to be quite cool. I couldn't have done it so easily if you hadn't co-operated.'

'I am not a star yet!' Julia smiled, tilting her head, 'Haven't gathered enough ego to stroke yet! Wait till I get the break I am looking for Randolf! I will become the mother of all bitches!'

Randolf laughed out. So did Julia.

She leaned forward and looked into Randolf's eyes, 'I was just wondering Randolf... why don't you do some nude portraits of me?'

'Did you want to do this in the nude?' Randolf asked apprehensively.

'Oh no! I am not talking of this one. This one is just fine the way you did it. I want to pose nude for myself. Not for any magazine or whatever. Just a collection to appease my narcissistic instincts you can say. And maybe to show to some close friends of mine.'

'Ah I see! You want to please your boyfriend.' Randolf chuckled.

'Oh no! Not him!' Julia said with a wave of her hand, 'He would be the last person I'd like to show. I'll do it for me only. And for you.' Julia lowered her voice to make it sound sexy.

'Me?' Randolf raised his brow.

'Why, won't you like to shoot me in the nude?' Julia asked, her eyes fixed at Randolf.

Randolf felt his heart gathered pace. Is this a proposal or an invitation?

'Yes Randolf?'

Before Randolf could reply Julia's cell rung. She picked it up and went inside the studio. Randolf realized it was Kevin, Julia did not want her boyfriend to know that she was still with him.

A couple of minutes later she returned with a frown above her brows.

'Was it Kevin?' Randolf asked.

Julia nodded.

'He is insisting it should be the way he wants. He had invited the editor and the creative director at the Sheraton Tuesday evening. He wants me to bring the photos with me, the way he wants it. Seminude.'

Randolf said nothing. Julia too remained silent, a distinct irritability appearing on her face.

'We can do it,' Randolf said finally, 'You want to pose nude too.'

'I want to do it for myself, not for him!' Julia snapped, 'And surely not for this one. This should remain the way you had done. I want you to come with me at Sheraton.'

Randolf noticed a steely resolve in Julia's face. Is she preparing for a showdown?

'Ok, as you wish,' he shrugged, 'I will bring out the prints tomorrow.'

****

Randolf watched the faces around the table. The tension in Julia was palpable, she was sitting straight, her body firm, eyes fixed at her boyfriend. Kevin Smith was expressionless, but a firmness had appeared in his jaw line as his eyes rolled over the photographs. The other two men had a common look on their faces. That of satisfaction and eagerness combined. The drama was building up, Randolf thought.

'Excellent!' Uttered Douglas Jardin, the editor of Citygirl as he looked at Randolf. 'What do you think Patrick?' He turned towards the Patrick Green, the creative head.

Patrick Green nodded his heads a few times and looked at Randolf and Julia.

'Indeed! Job well done young man!'

Randolf smiled and looked at Julia. She was smiling satisfied and pensive at the same time, her eyes going back to Kevin.

'What do you think dear?' She asked, her voice trembling a bit.

Kevin looked up to Julia and kept looking without blinking, his face as indifferent as it was throughout. Then he turned sideways and signaled the waiter to bring the bill.

'Which ones you liked best?' Randolf asked Jardin and Green ignoring Kevin.

'I like this set.' Green laid a group of ten photographs on the table. They were the ones of Julia in the red sari, with and without a black rimmed cap on her head. Wrapping the sari around her body like a sheet and unwrapping it too, she looked extremely sensual exposing parts of her naked shoulder and arms. The light fell upon her in such a manner that parts of her were illuminated highlighting the details of her skin including the pores, while the rest of her were in darkness.

'Me too.' Said Jardin. 'We will be publishing this in our next issue.'

That's cool. Randolf thought. He did not expect it to be so soon.

'We hope to work with you on a regular basis Randolf,' Jardin said. 'Are you willing?'

'It'll be my pleasure Sir.' Randolf smiled.

'You young lady,' Jardin turned to Julia, 'This lad has brought out the best in you. You look absolutely stunning. The whole town will be talking of you in a few days from now, I have no doubt about it.'

Julia blushed and once again looked at Kevin whose jaws hardened even more.

CHAPTER

The rest of the building was in darkness. Only one window on the upper floor was lit up. Kevin wondered what was going on behind the curtains. He looked at his watch. Nine-thirty. For the last one and a half hours he had been sitting inside his car, waiting. For what he did not know. He had been doing it for the three days. Leaving his office early he headed straight for Spencers Art Mart at Allen Avenue, in front of which he knew his girlfriend's silver Chevrolet would be parked, beside the gray Renault of Randolf Spencer. Some days he had to wait for half an hour, some days for one hour before the two would come out of the front door. Julia would lift herself to her toes to kiss the tall photographer and they would remain locked for a minute. Then Julia would get into her car and drive off, and he would follow her to her apartment at Encino. And every time she would lie when asked where she had been in the evening or why her phone remained switched off. Her explanations and excuses were lousy at best, even she knew she had not been able to convince him. But still she would keep up the farce and would make no effort to camouflage the glow that had appeared on her face since she had formed rapport with that photographer.

Kevin took another sip from the vodka bottle that was now near empty. His head felt dizzy as he looked up once again. They were still inside. Doing what? Making love? Is she as adventurous with that bastard as she was with him once upon a time? Now she was nothing but a plastic doll in his bed, a sexy Barbie who would do everything told to her, but with an icy coldness that made everything meaningless. He was losing to this young photographer from New York. What is there in him that he lacked? The charm? The sweet smile? The youth? But he was rich, more rich than this brat could even dream of in the wildest of his dreams. The bastard!

And he had humiliated him. For the first time in his life his opinion had been dumped with such disdain. As if he was some fool offering some foolish advice. What did he say... 'not everybody is born with the gift of appreciating the sublime.' Sublime! My foot! The bastard!

Kevin took another gulp from the bottle. The front door had opened... Kevin's jaws hardened and his fist clenched as he saw Julia and Randolf kissing. It seemed like an eternity. Finally Julia let loose Randolf and got into her car. Kevin started his. He was about to press the accelerator when he noticed that Randolf too had boarded his car. He decided to follow Randolf, not Julia.

****

Randolf brought down the window glasses to the full as he drove along the Pacific Coast Highway. He needed some fresh air to get rid of his fatigue. It had been a long day. He had to do some minute photoshopping to the shots that were selected for Citygirl and that took him the whole morning and afternoon. Julia came at four and the session began. This was the third straight day he was shooting her in the nude. He had taken hundreds of shots of her in every possible position but had not been able to satisfy the woman yet, she was craving for more. Not shots, but for the kicks she got from exhibiting her naked self in front of the camera, and the man behind it. And that was not all. She needed more. After every session she

204

came forward and drew him into her.

He did enjoy her company doing his best to satisfy her, both on and off camera but the excitement of the first day had not only diminished on the third, it had been replaced by fatigue and a feeling of emptiness. Every time he had held Julia in his arm this evening he thought of Oindrilla and her thought created a longing inside his heart that not even the sexiest overtures from this lustful diva could fulfill. That sex is dry without love he had felt no more intensely than he felt today. All the while he was in Julia's arms he thought of the all the afternoons he had spent in his Lexington Avenue apartment in the warm nearness of the Indian girl whom he loved. She was shy in her inherent Indian modesty, not at all adventurous like the wannabe Hollywood star, but still the satisfaction he got from her was hundred times better. It was because they had their hearts involved, here it was only the flesh. He was getting sick of it... Oindrilla hadn't called. He had no idea whether she came back from India or not. Or her mother. Deborah hadn't called yet, she would have if Oindrilla had returned. Should he call now, Randolf wondered, Oindrilla's home? Her father would be there. What's wrong in calling...?

Holding the steering with his left hand, Randolf brought out his mobile phone with his right. He pressed the scroll keys to get to the number. Suddenly he felt a bang and the phone flew from his hand... something hit the car on the left flank! Randolf lost control for a moment then regained by clutching the steering with both hands. There is a car to his left. A black BMW, its windows covered in dark glasses.

'F*** you!' Randolf yelled at the invisible driver. He pressed on the accelerator to brush past the car.

But the BMW caught up in a matter of seconds and swerved against the flank of his car. And again. Randolf realized he had come dangerously near to the edge of the road. He braked to slow down. But before he could bring his car out of the edge, the BMW hit again. This time so hard that Randolf could no longer maintain control. The car skidded and toppled over.

CHAPTER
NINETEEN

The door remained closed. Amy did not know when it would open. In the last one week it had rarely opened. And when it did the person who came out was not the girl she knew all her life. Oindrilla had changed. Six weeks in India had changed her daughter. She had become quieter and withdrawn, speaking only when spoken too. She sat on the dining table and ate in silence, engrossed in her own thoughts. It was not sign of any depression, Soham had assured, only mental fatigue. She would recover on her own. But a week had passed, she had shown no signs of opening herself up. Amy felt a deep pang inside her heart. Did she lose her daughter forever? The thought loomed over her all day and night like a heavy dark cloud. But at least her girl had returned home, she told herself again and again. That was no less consolation.

She was so ecstatic to hear her voice the evening she called. She was strolling in the terrace of her brother-in-law's house, her mobile phone was lying on the chair. When it rang and she saw the number on the dial, she could not recognize it, thought it was a wrong number that had been bothering her for sometime. In her dilemma whether to receive it or not she pressed a wrong switch and the call got disconnected. But seconds later it rang again. This time she received it right. There was silence on the side but a commotion could be heard on the background, people were shouting. 'Hello... Hello' she had repeated several times and with no reply coming she got irritated and thought of disconnecting when suddenly Oni's voice came from the other side. 'I am coming home Ma! I am coming home!' There was passion in her voice that felt like tears. Before she could say anything the call got disconnected. She waited and waited for her phone to ring again but it didn't. Then she tried herself. It was an Indian cell number, the 2 after 98 denoted that it was a Mumbai number. She tried several times but every time a female voice said, 'the number you are trying to call is busy. Please call after some time.' She tried again, after little time, but this time the voice said, 'the Hutch mobile phone you are trying to reach is switched off.' And it had remained switched off ever since. And her other phone too. Ever since she came back home Oni's phones had not rung even once.

Her phone had rung again. This time it was Soham. He said that Oni had called him too minutes back, and she was coming back home.

The relief was so overwhelming that she could no longer stand on her feet. It felt like a stone that was choking everything, every thought, every emotion of hers were being lifted suddenly. Six weeks of pent up tension suddenly dissipated in a second, being replaced by an overwhelming emotion of joy, relief and ecstasy. She had dropped to the chair and tears came out in unstoppable torrent. Ajay's wife who was instructing the gardener at the other end of the terrace came running. Hearing the news she grasped her with both hands and shared her emotion. For the first time she felt warmth in the woman from whom she had got nothing but indifferent coldness in the last few days.

She rang Calcutta to give the news to Avinash and Shruti. They were euphoric. Shruti said she would go to the Kalighat temple and pay her offering to the mother goddess that she had promised to do if Oni came back.

Sujoy came back from office late evening and hearing everything he suggested that they should go to the airport and look for Oindrilla. They went to the airport - Sujoy, his son and Amrita - and enquired about all the flights leaving for New York. To her utter disappointment they found out that Oindrilla had left in a Lufthansa flight minutes before they reached the airport.

It was a long flight back that seemed almost never ending. It was Soham who opened the door. She saw Oindrilla coming down the steps, she ran. Hugging her daughter as tightly as she could she cried and cried. She wanted to say something but all her words got washed in tears. Oindrilla did not cry but she held her mother tight, very tight. That was enough for her. Her daughter was back home and in her arms. She never felt happier ever before in her entire life.

But now she felt sad again. Her daughter had returned, but only in her body. The sprit was gone. And she had locked herself up in a shell ever since, a shell transparent enough to see that she was no longer resentful, but opaque enough to halt any attempt of reconciliation. So much so that she couldn't even bring herself to knock the door and ask her girl if she'd like to taste the pineapple ice cream she had so lovingly made for her.

Inside her room Oindrilla lay on her bed looking at the nothingness of the ceiling. She felt hungry but didn't want to get up and go to the kitchen. An overwhelming lethargy had taken her into its grip, infiltrating her mind too, frosting even her thoughts. Once in a while it thawed and the image of Sadiq lying dead on a pool of blood flashed before her eyes and she writhed on her bed to shut the thought off. She wriggled even more to block Randolf out of her mind every time he appeared, and in the process was drawn into a cesspool of pain so acute that it numbed even her soul. But again the lethargy creeps in and frosts her thoughts and she felt tired and drained out, not willing to move an inch.

But now she had to get up. Her hunger was getting more acute than her lethargy, she had to fill her stomach with something solid. A couple of bananas lay on a plate upon her study table, her mother had left the bunch sometime in the morning when she was drinking tea in the living room. She had eaten a few throughout the day but now she didn't feel like eating bananas anymore. She needed to eat something more appetizing, her appetite making a comeback. Oindrilla took up the New York Times lying beside her. She had read the front page while having tea in the living room, brought the paper to her room to read the rest, but she had fallen asleep. She turned over the pages reading nothing in particular.

Amy sat on the kitchen table peeling potatoes. She would make aloo dum today. Oni liked aloo dum very much, especially if made spicy. But she did not know how much she would eat. She had eaten very little in last few days. She knew what was bothering Oni... She was responsible. She was responsible for everything. Only if she could be a bit flexible. It was not that she hadn't liked the lad. She liked Randolf, she really liked him, he was so good looking, and had an air of honesty in him. Her daughter had fallen in love with someone who had not scared her a bit. It could have been one of those tattood Americans with cropped hairs wearing sleeveless leather jackets and riding bikes. Randolf was so different, he looked just like a prince in that blue sherwani that he wore the day he came to this house with her parents, all eyes were upon him. They would look so good; Randolf in silk zari sherwani and Oindrilla in a Benarasi sari...

Oh! What rubbish she was thinking!

Amy brushed aside her musings and concentrated on the job at hand. After peeling she had to boil the potatoes in the pressure cooker. Then she had to fry them in oil adding spices.

She heard footsteps. Getting up from her chair she came out of the kitchen. Oindrilla hurrying down the steps! She was wearing a long coat and had her travel bag on her shoulders. Amy felt a jolt in her heart. Is she leaving again!

Oindrilla stopped seeing her. Then she came down and stood before her.

'Where are you going?' Amy asked in a trembling voice.

'LA. Randolf's hurt.' Oindrilla replied and handed to her the newspaper she was holding in her hand. Then she walked out of the front door in quick long steps.

Bewildered, Amy looked at the paper. A small piece of news was marked with a circle around it. One injured in LA car crash, the heading read.

CHAPTER
T W E N T Y

The plane was half empty. 'You can sit anywhere.' The airhostess in blue uniform had told her, smiling sweet.

But she would not sit anywhere. She would not even sit in seat 27F, the number that was printed on her boarding pass. She kept moving down the gangway looking right and left at the faces of the sitting passengers.

There she is... sitting by the widow her face pressed to the glass. She looked so pained, so tired... and so alone... What is she thinking ? Her love, lying at a hospital bed? Or her mother who had been so cruel to her, snatching away all the happiness from her life ?

She moved forward. She hadn't noticed her yet.

'Oni.'

Oindrilla turned. In a matter of a second Amy saw pain turning into disbelief and then into joy.

'Ma!'

Amy moved in. Sitting beside her daughter she hugged her as tightly as she could.

'We will bring Randolf home dear,' she whispered.

 Within moments she felt a torrent of tears drenching her bosom.